MY FAVORITE MISTAKE

A LOVE LIKE THAT NOVEL

R.L. KENDERSON

ISBN-13: 978-1-950918-22-5

Editor: Jovana Shirley, Unforeseen Editing, www.unforeseenediting.com
Cover image:
Photographer: J. Ashley Converse, J. Ashely Photography, www.facebook.
com/jashleyconversephotography
Model: Austin Loes
Designer: R.L. Kenderson at R.L. Cover Designs, www.rlcoverdesigns.com

MY FAVORITE MISTAKE

ONE

MADELINE

I WATCHED MY BOYFRIEND, Harris, pull a suit from his closet and frown.

"Did you hear what I said?" I asked from my seat on the end of his bed.

Harris walked over and laid his clothes over his traveling garment bag without taking a single glance in my direction.

"Harris?"

He looked up at me, startled, almost as if he'd forgotten I was even there.

Sadly, this had been the state of our relationship lately.

"What?" he asked.

"Friday night."

"What about Friday night?"

I ground my teeth together as I stopped myself from reaching over and strangling him. "My friends want to get together for my birthday."

I watched a variety of emotions cross Harris's face. In the year and a half we'd been dating, he'd never hidden the

1

fact that he didn't care for my friends, and I sat and waited for him to make up an excuse as to why we couldn't go.

Harris pursed his lips. "Why don't you and I go out to dinner on Friday instead?" He smiled at me, giving me one hundred percent of the Harris Starling charm. It was the Harris smile that had gotten me to go on a date with him. And it was the Harris smile that had gotten me to sleep with him.

But now, it did nothing for me.

I mentally rolled my eyes because I was not some business deal he had to make. And I didn't answer right away because I didn't want to say something snarky I'd regret.

I picked up my phone and texted my best friend, Griffin.

> Me: Guess what.

> Griffin: You won the lottery.

> Me: Ha! I wish. No. I called it. Harris is trying to convince me to ditch you guys on Friday and go to dinner with him alone.

> Griffin: Fucking prick. And you didn't call it. I did.

> Me: Technically, we both did.

> Griffin: What did you tell him?

I looked up from my phone to see Harris had moved over to his dresser and was pulling out socks and underwear. I hated his tighty-whities. I never found them attractive.

Boxers or boxer briefs were better.

Commando was the best.

My phone buzzed in my hand.

Griffin: You still there? What did he say?

"We're going to dinner on Saturday night," I reminded Harris.

He paused and turned around. "Hmm?"

I sighed. "We're having dinner on Saturday, remember? That's why I wanted to go out with my friends on Friday." My tone had gone from casual to firm as I had to remind him of our plans once again. This was not the first time he'd forgotten.

Guilt flooded Harris's face, and his brown eyes avoided mine.

"What?" I asked with full-on irritation now. I knew him well enough to know that whatever he was going to say, I wasn't going to like it.

"I'm leaving town."

I lifted an eyebrow and looked at his clothes and luggage strewn about his bed. "I know."

"No, I mean, I'm leaving on Saturday now instead of Sunday."

"It's Wednesday, and you're just telling me this now?"

He shrugged. *Shrugged.*

"You do realize, my birthday is on Friday? A birthday you promised to be in town for." It wasn't every day that your girlfriend turned thirty.

Harris's blond brow furrowed. "I thought that your birthday was on Saturday."

I dropped my face in my hand and rubbed my forehead. I was so tired.

My phone vibrated in my other hand, so I peeked at it.

Griffin: Dump his ass.

Keeping my head down, I shot back a quick message.

Me: You don't even know what he said.

Griffin: It wasn't good if you're not even telling me what he said.

Me: You're right. He doesn't even know what day my birthday is.

Griffin: Break it off. You deserve better. Besides, you're always whining about not getting any.

I chuckled. Griffin always had a way of making me smile.

And that was why he was my best friend.

Me: I don't whine.

But Griffin was right. Harris and I hadn't had sex in weeks. We hadn't had decent sex in months. And unfortunately, we'd *never* had great sex.

Maybe I did complain a lot. I would never admit to whining though.

"What's so funny?"

I looked up at Harris, standing there with his hand on his hip, judgment on his face.

He probably had a good guess as to who I was texting, and I was sure he didn't like it.

Griffin and Harris had never gotten along.

I lost all humor as I stood and looked Harris in the eyes. It wasn't hard, as he was only two inches taller than me.

"Don't worry about dinner on Friday or Saturday."

Harris cocked his head. "I don't understand."

"We're not going to dinner either night."

"Don't you want your birthday present?"

"From you?" I said as I headed for the bedroom door. "No."

I heard the dresser drawer close behind me and the click of Harris's dress shoes on his hardwood floor as he followed.

Thank God it'd never become *my* hardwood floor.

Harris had asked me to move in more than once, but I always had a reason to say no.

Now, I knew the reason was gut instinct.

"Madeline, I don't understand."

I grabbed my jacket and purse from the couch on my way to the front door without answering right away.

The man was undeniably clueless.

I yanked open the thick oak door and turned around as the cool autumn air hit my back. "I don't need your birthday present because I am giving myself the best one."

He frowned. "And what's that?"

I grinned. "I am getting rid of you."

"What?"

"It's over, Harris. I'm done."

A thousand pounds fell from my shoulders, and I felt freer than I had in months.

I turned toward the outside air and sucked in a deep breath before pulling on my coat.

Damn, it felt good.

"You can't break up with me."

I looked over my shoulder at Harris. "I just did. Have fun on your business trip. Please don't call me when you get back."

I stepped out onto the front stoop and closed the door behind me. "Good riddance," I muttered. I hit a button on my phone and lifted it to my ear.

"You got Griffin," a deep rasp said in my ear.

Hearing his voice made me realize I had made the absolute best decision. My bestie was going to be so proud of me.

"Hey."

"Hey. I was wondering if I was ever going to hear back from you."

"I did it."

"Did what?"

"I broke up with Harris."

Griffin laughed in disbelief. "You're shitting me."

I smiled at the sound of hope in his voice as I unlocked my car and got behind the wheel. "I'm serious."

"*About fucking time,*" Griffin said a little too loudly in my ear, and I pulled the phone back with a grin.

I heard his big boots hit the floor and then the creak of his office door opening. I pictured him walking the hallway to the main room of his bar.

"She dumped his ass," Griffin shouted to the room, and I heard a bunch of cheers erupt. He put the receiver back to his mouth and said, "Hear that? Everyone's excited for you."

Griffin had worked hard on opening his bar, and he had a steady stream of regulars who liked to hang out almost every night. They all knew about my boyfriend and how Griffin didn't like the guy.

I grinned. "Yeah, I heard."

"They all want you to come in, so they can buy you a drink," he told me.

I didn't know if that was true, but I didn't care. I could use one right about now. "I'll be there in ten minutes."

"See ya then, Mads."

TWO
GRIFFIN

THE SECOND MADELINE walked into my bar, I slid over a cold bottle of her favorite beer.

She took a long swig before she even sat down.

"Ahh…" she said as she pushed her dark blonde hair over her shoulder. "That tasted better than it should have."

I grinned. "It's the taste of being single."

She rolled her eyes. "And you would know."

"Hey," I said as I picked up a glass to dry it. "I'm not against relationships." I was just against relationships where my best friend dated assholes who thought they were better than other people.

"Then, why are you never in one?" Madeline asked with a sparkle in her brown eyes.

She liked to put me on the spot.

But the joke was on her because I wasn't embarrassed.

I shrugged. "I date. I've just never met anyone I wanted to get serious with."

She eyed me over her beer as she took another sip. "Mmhmm," she said knowingly.

"He's too busy sleeping around."

I turned my eyes to Albert, one of my regulars. He was in his eighties and was in my bar every afternoon. He said alcohol kept him young. I was pretty sure his liver might disagree, but I wasn't going to judge. After all, he never got wasted, and his moderate drinking habit helped pay the bills.

I spread my hands out onto the bar and leaned in. "And how would you know, old man?"

Albert wasn't wrong. I did like to have sex, and it wasn't always with the same woman.

But I didn't shit where I ate, which meant I never took a woman home from my bar. This was my place of business, and I wasn't going to jeopardize everything I'd worked so hard for. I didn't need rumors floating around that I slept with customers, and I didn't need someone getting clingy with me and wanting more than I had to give. It would look bad.

Plus, I found that the illusion of me and my bartenders being unattached kept the single women coming to my bar. And if single women came, the single men followed, and they were the ones who really brought in the money. My regulars who lingered through the week kept the lights on, but it was the Friday and Saturday night singles crowds that made it possible for me to pay for everything outside the bar, like food and clothes.

Albert scanned me up and down. "You remind me of when I was your age. Good-looking. You work out and own a business. You can't tell me the ladies don't like you."

Madeline laughed and leaned over to get closer to Albert. "You're right. Our friend here is an S-L-U-T."

I frowned at her.

She shrugged and sat up. "What? I'm not saying it's a bad thing. It's just a statement of fact." She took a drink. "I'm thinking of becoming a slut myself."

"Becoming?" I teased.

"Ha-ha, Griff. You're hilarious." She stuck her tongue out at me. "In case you forgot, I just got out of a year-and-a-half relationship."

"True. But you have to remember, I've known you forever. I remember how you were in high school and heard plenty of stories from college."

She smiled wistfully, as if she was reminiscing about the past. "Yeah, I had some good times."

"I like loose women." Albert sighed. "But they don't seem to like me much anymore these days."

While I laughed, Madeline almost choked on the beer she'd sipped on when Albert spoke, and she patted his hand after she was able to stop coughing. "Hang in there. I'm sure you'll find someone."

Not if he kept coming to my bar every day rather than putting himself out there, but I wasn't complaining.

I propped my elbows on the bar and moved in close to Madeline. "How are you doing? Really?" I asked in a low voice.

She picked at the label on her beer bottle before meeting my eyes. "I'm good. Really."

I raised my eyebrows.

She rolled her eyes. "Of course, I'm a little sad, but things hadn't been good with Harris for a long time. I only wish it hadn't taken me so long to realize it."

"So, what did you tell him?"

She snorted. "Well, after he told me he was going to be out of town for my birthday—"

I winced. *Jackass.*

"I told him not to worry about going out to celebrate Friday or Saturday."

"What did he say?"

"He asked if I still wanted my birthday present."

"And?"

She grinned. "I told him that I was already giving myself the best birthday present. I was breaking up with him."

I threw my head back and laughed. "I bet he loved that."

"Not so much."

I laughed some more, picturing Harris's face as she'd delivered her birthday line. I wish I could have been there.

"Aren't you the least bit curious as to what he got you for your birthday?"

Madeline scrunched up her nose. "After Christmas, no."

"Yeah, you're probably right."

Harris had gotten her a new vacuum after her other one broke. It was top of the line and expensive, but...*dude.*

"Even I'm not that clueless."

She wiggled her eyebrows at me. "So, what are you getting me for my birthday?"

"I read online that all women want is a dress with pockets, so..."

She laughed.

"Seriously though, I'm still waiting for you to text me your list."

Madeline always picked out her own presents, and I just

bought what she'd told me to. It made both of our lives easier.

She took a drink of her beer as someone on the other end of the bar flagged me down. I held up a finger in the universal sign to wait a second.

"I haven't decided what I want yet. I'll send you some ideas soon."

I straightened, walked around to her side of the bar, and put my arm around her in a half-hug. "Sorry about your breakup right before your birthday."

She rested her cheek on my chest. "Thanks, Griff. It's for the best though."

The same customer from the other end of the bar was starting to get impatient, so when she lifted her head, I kissed her on the temple. "I have to go help another customer. I'll be back."

THREE
MADELINE

GRIFFIN WENT to help another patron, and I took my phone out of my purse. I opened my calendar and began deleting all the things I had planned with Harris. After about the tenth event, I realized how many things I did for him. Only one thing on the calendar had been my request. My birthday dinner.

With every hit of the Delete button on my app, I felt like I could breathe a little bit more. I had no idea what I was going to do with all my free time, but I sure as hell knew I was going to do something that I wanted to do.

The door opened behind me, and I looked over my shoulder to see a hot guy walk in.

Ooh. Maybe I'd get laid in my free time.

I closed my eyes, remembering the last time I'd had really good sex. It had been too long.

Maybe the hot guy would be interested. Sure, it was the middle of the week, but maybe he wouldn't be against a quick one-night stand.

Unfortunately, I lifted my lids just in time to see him walk up to a woman at a table. I crossed my fingers, hoping she was his sister. He leaned down and kissed her.

Nope. She was definitely not related to him.

I clicked my tongue in disappointment and turned back around, only to come face-to-face with Griffin.

"*Ah.*" I slapped my hand against his hard chest. "You scared me."

He didn't budge.

"If you keep staring at my customers like that, you're going to scare them. Away."

I shrugged. "I can't help it if I saw a good-looking man. I haven't been single for over a year." I stuck out my lower lip. "I miss good sex, Griff."

He knew all about my bedroom troubles with Harris.

"Sorry, babe. Maybe I can help you get some on your birthday. But if we do, it's going to be somewhere that isn't my bar." His blue eyes bore into mine to get his point across.

I knew he didn't like his friends hooking up with customers, and I understood. If something went bad, it could reflect poorly on the bar. But it didn't mean he wasn't ruining my buzz.

"You're no fun."

He looked over at Albert, who was talking to another customer, and then back to me. "Well, Albert just told me he's looking for a woman, if you're interested."

"Ha-ha, you're so funny. You know my age limit is seventy-five."

He shuddered. "And now, I'm picturing you having sex with Albert. Gross."

"You brought it up."

"As a joke."

I took a sip of my beer and tilted my head. "Is it gross because of Albert or because of me?"

He cupped my neck and ran his thumb along my jaw. "Babe, you know it's not because of you. You're gorgeous. You know it wasn't you who I said gross about."

I grinned. "Just making sure."

He shook his head. "Minx."

I laughed. "I just had to check if I still had it."

He looked me up and down in a way that made me understand how he got women to fall at his feet. "Always."

It also didn't hurt that my best friend was over six feet tall, handsome, and muscular. He had brown hair and had recently begun sporting a beard, which women seemed to love; the contrast of his dark hair made his blue eyes stand out. I'd also seen him in his underwear. He had a big dick. His suggestive looks were just icing on a very sexy beefcake.

"Damn, Griff." I jokingly fanned my face. "You're not so bad yourself."

He chuckled. "The only difference is, I know I still have it."

I playfully pushed his chest again because I was beginning to feel hot, and this time, he stood and backed away.

"It's a good thing I know you don't actually have a giant ego."

He shrugged. "You know I hate that self-centered shit."

"Yeah, I do."

Griff's older cousin had gone to our high school and was a narcissistic asshole. He was popular while being a bully to those weaker than him. Griffin hadn't been one of his victims, but the two of them didn't get along. Griffin had been popular, too, and played on the varsity hockey team, yet he'd never picked on anyone, and he didn't approve of anyone who did.

He eyed my almost-empty bottle. "You want another?"

"Why not?" My plans had been canceled the second I broke up with Harris. I might as well hang out with Griffin for a bit.

Unfortunately for me, the beer was going down too easy, and I realized that I needed to eat something, or I was going to feel horrible at work the next day. I worked in human resources. It would be highly frowned upon of me to show up hungover at work.

I spotted the evening bartender, Mitch, coming in from the back, and I was about to ask Griffin if he wanted to grab something to eat while I waited for my buzz to wear off when our friend Troy showed up.

"Hey, Madeline. What are you doing here?" he said. "If I had known, I would have brought Christina with me."

"Isn't she doing some wedding planning stuff tonight with her sister?" I asked.

"Yeah, but they could have done that another night."

"It's okay. Coming here was a last-minute thing."

I saw Griffin reach for his coat, and I knew he wasn't going upstairs to his apartment over the bar since he didn't need to go outside to get there.

"I didn't realize you had plans," I said.

Griffin shrugged his arms into his jacket. "Nothing fancy. We're going to grab some food and go shopping for a computer. I promised him I'd help him look."

"I get it, and I don't expect you to cancel your plans

because of me. But I don't think I can drive home yet. Do you mind if I head up to your place and order takeout?"

He smiled at me like my question was ridiculous.

"Thanks, Griff." I looked over his shoulder at the chalkboard on the wall as I slipped off my stool. "Oh, and my favorite color is teal."

When Griffin had begun making plans to open his bar, I'd jokingly told him to call it My Favorite Place. We lived in a suburb of Minneapolis, where it was close enough to go downtown to do things but far enough away that it had a small-town feel. I thought it would be funny for people to tell their friends they were going to their favorite place to drink when it was really the name of the bar.

He'd liked it so much that he actually named it that. And so, now, every day, he wrote a question on the wall, asking someone what their favorite fill-in-the-blank was. Sometimes, it was a more in-depth one, like: *WHAT IS YOUR FAVORITE QUOTE?* Today, it was an easy one: *WHAT IS YOUR FAVORITE COLOR?*

"I already knew that," he told me. "And you're welcome to my place anytime, babe. But you already know that too." He looked over at Mitch, who was walking from the back of the building. "Everyone's being taken care of right now. But keep an eye on Albert."

Albert looked over at Griffin upon hearing his name.

"He likes loose women," my best friend added loudly.

Everyone in the bar cracked up, and I headed upstairs to Griff's apartment.

I had my own key, so I let myself in, and I immediately ordered delivery from the Chinese food place close by.

I then turned on Griffin's TV and pulled up Netflix. I'd

forgotten how much I liked hanging out at his place, and I hadn't realized until now how much I'd kept myself away because Harris didn't like him.

Such a shame that I'd let a man do that to me. It'd happened so gradually that it snuck up on me. I hadn't made it past the bar in at least a month. Before that, I thought I had come upstairs for all of five minutes.

I knew that it was hard for men I dated to understand that Griffin and I were best friends, but some accepted it easier than others. It always helped when my best friend and my boyfriend got along with each other.

In the future, if the guy I dated didn't like my best friend, I wasn't going to keep him around. If Griffin were a female, it wouldn't be a problem, and I really hated double standards.

As I kicked off my shoes and rested my feet on the coffee table, I thanked myself once again for calling my relationship with Harris quits.

Fifteen minutes later, my food arrived. I ate way too much and almost fell asleep on the couch. With my last bit of energy, I went into Griffin's room and pulled out some sweatpants and a T-shirt from his dresser. I brushed my teeth with the spare toothbrush I kept at his place, and then I slid into his king-size bed and sent him a text.

> Me: I'm sleeping over. Don't bring any women home.

He had two bedrooms but only one bed. The other room was filled with workout equipment. And there was always the couch, but we'd been sharing each other's beds for sleeping for as long as I could remember. I knew he wouldn't care if I stayed over.

Griffin: Oh, darn. Hold on. I have to cancel the threesome I was going to have tonight. The ladies are going to be so disappointed.

Me: Tell them hi for me.

Griffin: They said to tell you to go to hell.

Me: LOL.

Griffin: Troy and I are almost done here anyway. I'll be home soon.

Me: Okay. Please don't wake me.

Griffin: You couldn't pay me to wake you.

I thought of myself as a fairly nice person, but wake me up when I wasn't ready, and even I knew I was a bitch. It always took me about ten minutes to return to normal.

Me: Ha. I'll see you in the morning then.

Griffin: Okay. Night.

Me: Night.

I turned my screen black and set my phone on the night-stand. I was out as soon as my head hit the pillow. The only thing that vaguely pulled me from slumber was the sound of feet shuffling on the floor and the bed dipping down beside me.

Griffin was home, but he had the good sense not to disturb me.

And I fell asleep once more.

FOUR
GRIFFIN

THE SOUND of Madeline's phone pulled me from sleep. I knew it was her phone and not mine because I would never have a ringtone that played Taylor Swift.

"Hello?" she said from the other side of the bed.

"Hi, honey."

Since the only sound in my place was the air blowing out of the vent in the floor, I could hear Madeline's mom, Nora, perfectly.

I opened my eyes and saw Madeline roll onto her back.

She ran her hand across her face. "Hey, Mom. What's up? You're calling pretty early."

I looked over my shoulder at my alarm clock to see that it wasn't quite seven.

"Oh, I'm sorry. Did I wake you? I thought you'd be up for work already."

"It's okay. I was half-awake. I do need to get up and get ready anyway."

"I'll make this quick then. On Sunday, it'll be just you

for dinner, right? I think you said Harris was going out of town. I wanted to make sure before I went to the store."

"Yeah, it's just me."

"So, Harris is going out of town?"

"He is. But it doesn't matter because we broke up."

"*Hallelujah.* Your father is going to be so happy."

Madeline scoffed while I stifled a laugh.

"Mom, really?" she said as she looked at me and pointed to her phone. *Are you hearing this?* she mouthed.

I nodded with a grin.

I'd known Nora Campbell as long as I'd known her daughter, and she was like a second mother to me. And it was the same with Madeline and my mom. Madeline and I were only children, so I thought our mothers liked having both of us around. I thought our dads liked it, too, but they'd both come from a generation where men didn't show their feelings as much.

"I'm sorry, honey. I meant to say, this is unfortunate news. I hope you're doing okay."

"Too late." She rolled her eyes. "If you and Dad didn't like Harris, why didn't you tell me?"

"It's not that we didn't like him. We didn't like him for *you.* You two were all wrong for each other. But I knew it would eventually work itself out. I'm just glad it was sooner rather than later."

"Next time, just tell me how you feel, okay?"

"Sure, honey," Nora said in a placating tone.

"I don't believe you."

Nora laughed. "You'll just have to trust me. We can talk about this more on Sunday. I'll let you go, so you can get ready for work. I need to head out the door soon too."

"Okay." Madeline sat up. "I'll see you on Sunday."

"See you then. I love you, honey."

"I love you too." She hung up the phone and looked over at me. "I can't believe her. She had a mini celebration about my breakup."

"I don't blame her. Your mom was right. Harris was all wrong for you."

Reaching behind her, Madeline picked up the pillow she'd just been resting her head on and threw it at me.

I caught it before it could hit me in the face and tucked it under my head.

"I'm disowning you both," she said as she got out of bed.

"No, you're not. You love us all too much."

She snorted and pulled my T-shirt she'd borrowed over her head.

The two of us were close and had never done anything sexually intimate in all our years as friends, but I sometimes thought Madeline forgot I was a man. I had a perfect profile view of her perky C-cup breasts, and best friend or not, it didn't stop me from wondering what her pink nipples would taste like in my mouth.

I looked away and subtly adjusted my dick under the covers. I was a red-blooded male after all, and a beautiful set of tits were still a beautiful set of tits, no matter who the owner was.

When I turned back in her direction, she had thankfully already put on a bra and was pulling her shirt down over her smooth stomach.

Unfortunately, my borrowed sweatpants were next. And even with her underwear covering her bottom half, it didn't stop me from wondering what her pussy tasted like too.

I groaned low in my throat.

I needed to stop thinking about sex.

I blamed it on my lack of caffeine and the fact that I'd just woken up.

I pushed off my comforter and got out of bed, hoping my T-shirt was low enough to cover my hard-on.

"Do you want coffee?" I asked her.

Madeline bit her bottom lip and wiggled her eyebrows. "Are you happy to see me, or is that a gun in your boxers?"

"You are such a dork," I said as I walked past her and headed for the kitchen. "I take back my coffee offer."

She laughed as she followed me. "But I'm your dork, Griff." She plopped her butt down on the stool at my counter. "Now, bring me coffee, Ol' Hard One."

I busted out laughing as I shook my head. Madeline could always make me smile. She really was a dork sometimes and didn't care if others thought so too. It was one of the things I loved about her.

I grabbed the coffee grounds from my cupboard. "How are you feeling this morning?" I asked seriously. "Besides your mom and her revelation, are you regretting the breakup?" I grabbed the pot and started filling it with water.

"Not at all." She pointed to her phone on the counter. "Do you know he didn't text me once after I left?"

I winced.

"Don't feel bad. It only shows me how he really felt about me. Also, it shows me how I really felt about him because I'm relieved. I do not want another Elliot."

"I agree."

Madeline had dated Elliot for only four months, and the guy wouldn't stop texting her for months afterward. I finally tracked him down and had a few words with him. Nothing threatening. I simply explained to him, guy-to-guy, how his constant messaging looked to a woman and how it was never going to convince her to give him a second chance. I didn't know if he'd quite gotten it, but he'd stopped bothering Madeline after that.

I pushed the On button and opened the fridge to get the coffee creamer she refused to go without. I noticed a couple of boxes of Chinese food in the fridge, so I pulled one out to inspect it.

It was Madeline's leftovers.

I opened the other box.

It was Hunan chicken. My favorite. And it was filled to the brim.

I looked over the top of the fridge. "Did you get me Chinese food?"

"Of course. I figured you could have it for lunch or something."

"Are you sure you don't want to take it to work?"

She smiled. "I'm sure. I'll take my leftovers though."

I pulled her box out and set it on the counter. "So you don't forget it."

"Thanks."

"So, now that you're single, are you changing the plans for Friday? Are we going to go downtown and hit up a club?"

"Eh." She shook her head. "I think I'd rather stay around here. Plenty of bars to choose from. My only request is, we go somewhere with a patio. It's supposed to be nice this weekend, and it might be the last few warm nights until spring."

The suburb where my place was located was on a two-block radius with several other bars. Some had thought it was crazy to start a business with so much other competition, but it actually worked in our favor. People could go from bar to bar by walking, and they didn't need to worry about drinking and driving.

I liked it because I was close enough to my own place in case something came up. I had good staff who had earned my trust, but one never knew when they would need me to step in.

Madeline narrowed her eyes. "Scratch that. I have two requests. You have to drink and have fun. Your baby can last without you one night."

"My baby?"

"Yeah, your bar. It's practically your baby."

I laughed.

"That's not an answer." The coffeemaker beeped as she put her hand over mine. "Promise me, we're going to have fun."

I used my free hand to make an X on my chest. "I cross my heart. We'll have fun."

She sat back with a satisfied smile. "Good. I have a feeling this might be my best birthday yet."

FIVE
MADELINE

I WALKED into My Favorite Place as the sun was starting to set. This time of year, it wouldn't take long for it to be dark outside.

"Hey, Madeline," Mitch greeted me from behind the bar. "Happy birthday."

I grinned. "Thanks, Mitch." I scanned the room. "Where's Griffin?" I narrowed my eyes back toward his office. "Please tell me he's not working still. I told him I'd be here at seven."

"Nah. He's upstairs, getting ready. While you wait, do you want your free birthday drink?"

I laughed. All my drinks at Griff's place were free. "Sounds great."

"You want your usual beer?"

"Nah. It's my birthday. Surprise me."

When Mitch smiled, there was an extra glint in his eye.

"It'd better taste good, or I'm telling on you to the boss."

"You got me," he said as he pulled out a glass.

"Got you how?" Casey, the other bartender on duty tonight, asked.

Fridays were much busier than weekdays, so there were usually at least two bartenders and two servers working. And Griffin filled in wherever he was needed when he was there. I hoped they had enough people scheduled tonight because I was going to be upset if they called my best friend away from my birthday celebration.

"She figured out I was going to give her something nasty to drink," Mitch told her.

"Never trust a man," Casey told me.

"Noted," I said. I leaned forward. "Listen, Griffin promised me that he was going to drink and have fun tonight. Do you think you two can handle the bar and not pull him away? I know he's usually here to help on the weekends, but tonight's special."

Casey smiled. "Don't worry. The boss scheduled us an extra bartender and server tonight."

My heart warmed. "He did?"

"He did," Mitch said and slid over my drink. "And he told us not to call him unless we also had to call 911 at the same time."

"Thanks. I was really worried he'd be called away." It had happened more than once when we tried to go somewhere that wasn't Griffin's bar, including on his own thirtieth birthday. "And he's always worried about all of you."

Casey and Mitch frowned.

"In a good way," I quickly added. "He feels guilty when he's not here, helping out."

The two seemed to accept my answer, and I swiftly

picked up my drink before they said something that put me on the spot.

I took a big sip. "*Woo.* That is strong." I shook my head to clear it.

Mitch smiled. "It's good, isn't it? I made it up myself."

I took another drink and nodded my head. It wasn't that good, but he seemed so proud that I didn't want to say anything to hurt his feelings.

Thankfully, I didn't have to come up with any lies about how great his concoction was because Casey put two fingers between her lips and whistled.

I turned to see Griffin walking toward us from the back of the bar. He had on a long-sleeved black henley and dark jeans. His beard was freshly trimmed—just the right length, if you asked me—and his hair was fixed. He was smiling, and his blue eyes lit up when he saw me.

When he reached me, he pulled me into his arms and hugged me. "Happy birthday, Mads."

My nose was in his neck, and I couldn't help but notice how good he smelled. Just a hint of cologne and a whole lot of man.

"Thank you," I said, my lips brushing against his skin.

I pulled away as a strange feeling sent flutters through my stomach.

I smiled at him and tugged at his shirt. "My, don't you look pretty sexy tonight?" I playfully told him, ignoring the unusual feeling in my belly.

He grabbed my hand and spun me around. "Look who's talking," he said.

I looked down at my purple top and black skirt. "I felt like looking pretty on my birthday," I said.

"Babe, you're going to have men falling at your feet."

I grinned. "I can only hope."

Griffin laughed and pointed to my drink. "You want to finish that before we go?"

I opened my eyes wide and slightly shook my head. "Yes, I do," I said out loud.

Griffin reached over and grabbed the glass. Before I could stop him, he swallowed the rest of the drink down.

He coughed a few times when he was finished. "Holy shit, Mitch. What did you put in here, lighter fluid?"

"Hey, Madeline said she liked it."

"She was lying."

Mitch's eyes flew to mine.

I winced and shrugged. "I'm sorry."

"Please don't ever make that again," Griffin told him.

Mitch started muttering something I couldn't hear, but Griff didn't seem concerned.

"You ready to go?" he asked me. "When are we meeting everyone?"

"I told them seven thirty, so we should probably go." I had decided we should start at the bar farthest from Griffin's place and make our way back here.

Unless I found a guy tonight for some reason, I would be sleeping in Griffin's apartment again. There was no way I was driving home.

When we reached our destination, it was busier than I had thought it would be.

"Why don't you go and see if you can find everyone? I'll get us drinks."

Griffin agreed and headed toward the back of the room, where there were more tables.

I parked myself at the bar to wait for one of the two bartenders to make their way over to me. I had my eyes toward Griffin to see if he'd found our friends. It looked like he might have found them because he smiled and stopped walking. He met my eyes and waved to make sure I saw where he was, and I nodded back.

"Oh my God," a woman said behind me.

I thought maybe she was speaking to me, and I was about to turn around, but I stopped when I heard her friend respond.

"What?"

"I just saw Griffin Davis."

The two women had my full attention. Using my hair as a curtain, I turned my head slightly so that I could hear what they were about to say about my best friend.

"Who's that?" the second woman asked.

"A guy I dated a while back."

I closed my eyes to see if I could recognize the first woman's voice, but there was too much noise around us. Or there was the chance that I hadn't even met her.

I doubted it because Griffin didn't hide women from me, but there was a pinch in my chest at the thought that maybe he had done just that.

"Is this the guy with the cute dog or the guy who fucked you like a rock star?"

I already knew the answer because Griffin didn't own a

dog. Also, it wasn't the first time I'd heard that he was good in the sack.

"The latter." She squealed. "He was *so* good."

"I'm jealous," her friend said.

"I'm jealous of myself. Maybe after we get our drinks, I should go over and see if he'll give me a repeat performance," Woman One said.

Woman Two responded, but I didn't hear what she said because I was already walking away.

Griffin turned in my direction and frowned when he saw me. "What's wrong?"

I looked around him to see that he wasn't talking to our friends but to someone I didn't know.

"I want to go."

"Are you okay?"

"Yes." The truth was, I wasn't really sure what was wrong. I just knew I didn't want to stick around and have the woman take Griffin from me.

I mean, it was my birthday after all. And I didn't want my best friend to leave me.

I wasn't quite convinced of my reasoning. But I didn't have time to think about that right now.

"I want to leave."

"We just got here. Everyone else is on their way."

"We'll text them." I wrapped my fingers around his lower arm and squeezed. "Please."

"Of course, babe. It's your birthday."

A huge wave of relief washed over me, and I smiled.

Griffin shifted around. "Looks like we're leaving. Talk to you later."

His friends said good-bye, and he threw his arm around

my neck when he faced me again. "Let's go. Where are we headed?"

"Let's go two doors down. Remember how I said I wanted to sit outside? We should do that sooner rather than later in case it gets cold."

He laughed. "You could have just said that. I thought something bad had happened to you."

I forced a laugh. "Sorry to worry you."

As we walked out the door, I peeked at the bar to see if I knew who had been talking about Griffin.

At first, I didn't see a face that looked familiar, but then I saw Holly, and I had to hold in a laugh.

My best friend hadn't hidden a girl from me, and even better, I knew Griffin didn't like her.

And the best part was that he'd told me more than once that she was bad in bed.

Oh, Holly. There is no way Griffin is giving you a repeat performance.

SIX
MADELINE

GRIFFIN and I found a table outside with enough room to fit us and our friends. It was next to the fire burning in the outdoor fireplace. We had already picked up drinks and were just waiting for the others to show.

I checked my phone. "Christina said that she and Troy were only five minutes away. But it's been almost ten."

I looked to see Griffin shrug.

"They're probably parking."

"You're probably right." I smiled. "I'm so lucky I don't have to worry about that." I parked in the back of the building along with the employees.

Griffin leaned forward. "So, do you want to tell me why we really left the other bar?"

I looked away for a moment. There was no point in lying to my best friend. He knew me so well; I couldn't get away with it. But there was no way I was going to tell him about the weird feeling I'd had when I didn't even get it.

I turned back to him and sighed. "I saw Holly."

His brow furrowed. "Holly? The chick I dated for a couple of weeks, back a few months ago?"

"Yeah."

"So?"

"She said she wanted a repeat performance of you and her in bed."

He grimaced, and I couldn't help but laugh.

Griffin sat back in his chair. "I guess I should thank you then." He frowned. "Although that doesn't seem like quite the emergency you made it out to be when you ran up to me."

"I didn't run. I walked fast. And"—I shrugged a shoulder—"I suppose I didn't feel like sharing you on my birthday."

Or at all, a little voice said in my head.

Whatever. My brain didn't know what it was talking about.

"Does that make me a bad person?" I asked.

He smiled and took a drink of his beer. "Nah. I wouldn't want to share me either."

"Ha-ha-ha," I mock laughed. "What were you saying about ego the other night?"

Griffin didn't answer because our friends Troy and Christina came out of the back door and onto the patio.

"Happy birthday," they all yelled, and I felt my face heat from embarrassment.

"Happy birthday," a couple of strangers from the tables next to us called out.

"Thanks, everyone." I stood and gave Christina a hug as she reached the table.

35

She shoved a present toward me. "Here's your birthday present from Troy and me."

"Thank you." I grinned. "I can't wait to open it."

Christina and I had gone to college together while her now-fiancé, Troy, had attended the same university as Griffin. She had gone with me to visit my best friend and met Troy. They'd been dating ever since, and they were getting married in a few months.

A few seconds later, my coworker April and her boyfriend, JJ, walked outside.

April and I had clicked the first day she started working with me, and now, she was part of the group. And she'd been with her boyfriend for almost two years, so we had accepted him as one of our own too.

April gave me a hug. "Happy birthday."

"You already told me that at work today," I joked.

"Here's your present." She handed me a small gift-wrapped box.

"And you already brought cake to work. You didn't have to get me anything."

She held her head high. "Yes, I did. Now, say *thank you* and sit down."

I laughed. "Thank you."

As I sat back down, Christina said, "Open mine first."

I picked up the gift bag and pulled out the tissue paper on the top. There were two items inside. I chose the box first and opened it.

My eyes flew up to my friend. "You got me the bracelet we saw when we were shopping? But when did you get it?"

She grinned. "When you were looking at other stuff."

"Sneaky," I said as I took the piece of jewelry out of the

box and put it on around my wrist. I held my arm to Griffin. "Will you clasp this for me?"

As he worked on my bracelet, I used my other hand to pull out the item in the bag. It looked like lipstick, but it was heavier than normal. When Griffin finished, I pulled off the cap. It was plastic.

"Twist it up," Christina said.

I did as she'd suggested, and it started vibrating.

I immediately busted out laughing. "Is this what I think it is?"

"It's a clit vibrator that you can carry with you wherever you go. I figured now that you and Harris were over, you might need it." Christina grinned.

Griffin held out his hand.

"Awesome." I turned it off and set it in Griffin's outstretched palm. "Thank you both."

Troy pointed to his fiancée. "It was all Christina. I don't buy sex toys for women other than her."

"Mine next," April said.

I unwrapped the box she had handed me earlier and opened the lid. Inside was a gift card to a local bookstore.

"I had the same idea Christina did, I guess."

I didn't understand.

"Take it out," April said. "There's another surprise underneath."

I took out the gift card to find another one for my favorite lingerie store.

"I thought you could go shopping for books and get yourself some pretty lingerie now that you're single. It's always nice to make yourself feel sexy again after a breakup."

I shook my head and smiled. "You two ladies are the best. Thank you."

I took the lipstick vibrator back from Griffin, who had been studying it, and the two gift cards and stuck all three in my purse.

"So, what did you get Madeline, Griff?" Christina asked.

He lifted up his hands. "Nothing yet. She still hasn't told me what she wants."

"Oh yeah, I kind of forgot after Wednesday. Yesterday, I went to Harris's while he was at work, and I picked up all the stuff I'd had there and left my key. And today, I was focused on tonight." I patted his knee. "I'll think of something for you to get me."

"You'd better because I'm not letting you top me with the gift you got me this year."

I had gotten Griffin a neon sign with the name of his bar.

"My gift wasn't that great."

"It is when I didn't get you anything."

I chuckled. "That's a fair point. Don't worry. I'm sure there is something out there that I want."

"Just make sure you pick something sexual and nonsexual," he joked, "since that seems to be the running theme."

"Ooh. In that case, I want the biggest dildo you can buy," I teased back.

Griffin snickered. "No. I am not buying a dildo."

"That's too bad," I said with fake disappointment. "Because I was going to buy you a pocket pussy next year."

He laughed and looked me in the eye. "Babe, I don't need a pocket pussy when I get plenty of the real thing."

SEVEN

MADELINE

A COUPLE HOURS LATER, the six of us were laughing and joking around, and I was feeling pretty good. I was enjoying my birthday buzz.

Unfortunately, all that drinking made me need to use the ladies' room.

I pushed back my chair. "I'm going to go to the restroom. Anyone coming with me?"

"I'm fine," April said.

"Me too," Christina said.

Griffin pushed back his chair. "I'll go with you. I could go to the bathroom, and I'm out of beer. The servers haven't come around for a while."

The two of us walked inside and went to opposite sides of the hall. There was a short line to the ladies' room but none to the men.

Figures.

"You want to meet me at the bar when you get out?" he asked me.

"Yeah. Will you order me a beer?"

"Will do."

By the time I made it in and out, about fifteen minutes had passed. I had to wonder if Griffin had even waited for me.

I looked around the room toward the bar and saw his dark head sticking out of the crowd toward the front, and I smiled. He hadn't left me.

Weaving my way through the crowd, I wasn't prepared for what I saw when I reached him.

Holly had found Griffin.

And the poor guy looked like he'd rather be anywhere but there.

I slid up beside him and moved in close. "Hey, Griff." I looked at Holly. "Hey..." I bit my lip, pretending like I couldn't remember her name. It was petty of me, but that uneasy feeling was back, and I blamed her.

"Holly," she said, clearly unhappy to see me.

I snapped my fingers. "Right." I grinned. "Hi, Holly. How are you?"

She smiled stiffly. "Fine. If you don't mind, Griffin and I were talking."

I didn't have a good response for this, but I didn't need one.

Griffin put his arm around me and tugged me close. "Sorry, Holly. It's Madeline's birthday, and I promised to spend the night with her."

Holly rolled her eyes and sighed. "Yeah, I shouldn't be surprised," she said to herself more than to us. She looked at the two of us and shrugged. "Your loss," she said to Griffin and walked away.

Once she was out of earshot, the two of us started laughing.

"*Your loss*," I mimicked. "If she only knew."

Griffin snorted.

He still had his arm around me, and he pulled me into a semi-hug, so we were chest to chest. "I owe you."

I clutched his sides and enjoyed the feel of him under my hands. He felt and smelled delicious. "Yeah, you do."

"I'm going to have to get you an extra-big present now."

I laughed and rested my head on his chest as the bartender approached.

"Two beers," he said, and I felt the rumble of his deep voice next to my ear.

As I looked out into the crowd, my eyes landed in the corner of the bar, where a couple was making out. Actually, it looked like they were past making out and moving on to doing things they shouldn't be doing in public. The guy had his mouth on the woman's neck, and her head was thrown back in what was clearly an O face.

I looked up into Griffin's face as he paid the bartender and put his wallet back in his pocket.

"I want that," I told him.

His brow furrowed as he looked down at me. "Want what?"

I nodded toward the couple. "That."

Griffin squinted off into the distance. His face changed to surprise. "Whoa. Those two need a room." He turned his head sideways. "What is he doing to her? Because she looks like she's…"

"Orgasming? Yeah, I know." I grabbed his chin and

turned his face toward mine. "I want that. For my birthday present."

This time, his eyebrows went up. "You want to have an orgasm in the bar?"

I chuckled. "No. I want to have an orgasm so good that I don't care where I am."

"That makes more sense." He seemed to think about it for a second. "I suppose I did offer to help you get some on your birthday, didn't I?"

I let go of his chin and ran my hand down his chest. "No, you don't understand. I don't want you to help me find someone to have sex with. I want *you* to have sex with me. I want you to fuck me so good that my legs shake when I come."

Griffin took a small step back. "Jesus, Madeline."

Well, this wasn't going how I'd thought it would. My best friend was usually all about sex and never seemed to be picky when it came to his partners. He loved women in all shapes, sizes, races, and ages. I never thought he would be against sleeping with me, but if his physical retreat meant anything, it was that he was not excited to have sex with me.

Still...*in for a penny, in for a pound.*

And thanks to the boost of confidence from the alcohol, I was able to finish my thought, but I didn't close the distance between us. He obviously needed his space.

"Look, I know you're good in bed." I scoffed and rolled my eyes. "I've heard more than one woman sing your praises. And I want that. It's not every day someone turns a decade older, and I'm thinking some mind-blowing sex is the perfect present," I said with a smile.

He sighed, and I knew I wasn't going to like what came

out of his mouth next. "I don't think that's a good idea, Mads. You and I are friends. You're my best friend. And I like it that way."

My smile fell. I realized he didn't want to ruin our friendship, but I was still hurt. He could have added that I was hot and he thought we'd have a good time, but it wasn't for the best. People had joked with us that they couldn't believe we'd never dated before. I always thought it was because we were such close friends, but it turned out, it might be because he wasn't attracted to me.

I forced myself to smile again, but I couldn't quite get it to reach my eyes. "It's okay. I understand." I picked up my beer. "Forget I said anything."

"I need a shot down here," Griffin yelled to the bartender.

And now, it seemed like he didn't want to even walk back outside with me. I hadn't meant to shake him up that much.

"Right. Well, I'll meet you back outside then," I told him.

"Madeline, wait," he said, but I had already turned around and was heading for the patio.

As I made my way through the bodies of people, I considered going back outside through the front door. The cool air would help me clear my head without facing my friends right away. As much as I understood Griffin's side, if our friends found out, I would be mortified. Rejection was still rejection even if it came from a good place.

Out of nowhere, someone bumped into me from behind, and my beer spilled onto my hand.

I turned around, ready to see who was being careless

and rude. The crowd was large, yet everyone else managed not to run into others. But I stopped when I saw a handsome man with a sincere, apologetic look on his face.

"I am so sorry about that. My rude friend seemed to forget we were surrounded by people." He handed me a napkin.

I changed my mind. He was very handsome.

"Apology accepted," I said as I wiped my hand clean.

"So, are you here with anyone?" he asked.

I smiled. For real this time. "I'm with friends. We're celebrating my birthday tonight."

"Happy birthday."

"Thank you."

"Do these friends include a boyfriend?"

I laughed. "Nope. I dumped him two days ago."

The guy laughed and stuck out his hand. "I'm Todd. And the asshole who pushed me is Clay."

"Hi, Todd. Hi, Clay. I'm Madeline."

"Sorry for the run-in," Clay said. "Happy birthday."

"Thanks," I said to Clay.

"Can I buy you a birthday drink?" Todd asked, still holding my hand. He looked down at my other hand and blushed. "I mean, I know you already have a full glass, but I can wait until you're finished."

How cute. The guy was flustered. Over me.

It was just the pick-me-up my confidence needed after Griffin's rejection.

"Thank you. I would lo—"

"She's with me."

I looked over Todd's shoulder as Griffin stepped around him and put his arm around me.

Todd immediately dropped my palm and held his hands up. "Sorry, man. She said she didn't have a boyfriend."

I sighed. "I don't. This is my friend Griffin. Griffin, this is Todd. Todd, Griffin."

Todd eyed Griffin warily even though I'd explained to him my relationship with Griffin. He looked at me. "Maybe some other time. You have a good night, Madeline. And happy birthday."

Todd and Clay walked away, and I gave Griffin a look.

"Thanks for that. Weren't you just telling me that you promised to help me get some on my birthday?"

His eyebrows rose. "That's it? We're not going to talk about what just happened between us?"

"No." I was still a little hurt, but I would get over it. Griffin was my best friend, and him rejecting me wasn't something to throw away our friendship over. I put my hand on his arm. "Let's just pretend like I never asked you what I asked you, okay?"

"But I didn't even give you—"

"There you are."

We both turned to see Troy standing beside us.

"Do you care if we head down to My Favorite Place?" he asked me. "It's getting cold out there."

Christina popped up next to Troy. "I say we stop at the bars on the way down to Griffin's place for a birthday shot before we end up there."

I would have thought it was an excellent idea a half hour ago, but I no longer wanted to get drunk and crash at Griffin's apartment. I could already feel how awkward it would be to lie there next to him. He'd probably be afraid I was going to jump him, and I would be afraid that he was afraid I was going to jump him.

I was sure the whole asking Griffin to sleep with me would blow over but not within a few hours; it was best I started sobering up, so I could go home.

"Actually, let's just head down there anyway. I don't really feel like stopping at a bunch of places."

"It's only two other bars," Christina pointed out.

"I know, but let's just go to Griffin's."

She shrugged. "It's your birthday." She looked down at my hand. "You'd better finish your beer first. I'll go tell April and JJ we're taking off."

Damn. I'd forgotten I still had a full drink.

I lifted the glass to my mouth and started chugging. It wasn't until I was about halfway finished that I thought to ask Troy if he wanted it.

"You want the rest of this?" I asked him.

"Sure. We're planning to Uber home, so I might as well."

I looked at Griffin. "You'd better finish your beer too," I said, eyeing his half-full glass.

Troy raised his hand. "I'll drink that, too, if you don't want it."

Griffin pushed the glass into Troy's chest and grabbed my hand. "Let's go outside. We can talk while we wait."

I didn't want to talk. It was my birthday night, and we were supposed to be having fun.

I was about to tell him that we could talk tomorrow, but I heard April yell from behind me, "Wait for us."

I laughed and turned around until all four of our friends caught up.

"Here's your purse," April said, handing it to me.

"Thanks." I had been so caught up in what had happened with Griffin that I'd almost left it out there.

"Aww, Griffin's holding Madeline's hand," Christina said when she looked down at our hands.

I rolled my eyes and tried to drop his hand.

He seemed determined to hold on because his grip tightened.

"When are you two going to date already?" April asked.

Oh jeez, April, not tonight.

"I just downed half a beer. Griffin wants to make sure I don't trip and fall down," I joked.

"Shall we go then?" Christina asked.

"Let's go."

We walked out of the building, and I gave my best friend a look once we were outside.

He smiled at me, so I felt like maybe my mishap wasn't the worst thing in the world.

But Griffin still held my hand the whole way down to his bar.

EIGHT

MADELINE

WHEN WE GOT to My Favorite Place, Griffin immediately went behind the bar, which I supposed was inevitable. And despite the lecture I had given him earlier in the night about not working, I was kind of relieved he had split from the group.

Casey came out from behind the bar when she saw us and held out her arm. "Right this way, birthday lady."

I raised my eyebrows.

She dropped her hand. "Just come with me."

I laughed, and the five of us followed her. In the corner was a round booth that fit several people. It was the only one in the bar, and on top of the table, it had a sign that read *Reserved*.

"Griffin dropped us a text and told us to make sure the booth was yours," Casey explained.

"Aw, that was sweet of him," Christina said and slid behind one side of the table.

Everyone else followed until I was last. I took a seat at one of the ends.

"What can I get everyone?" Casey asked. "I'll make up your drinks and have one of the servers bring them over."

The group put in their orders, and then Casey turned to me.

I leaned close to her. "I'll just have a water," I whispered.

She put her hand to her ear. "I'm sorry. I can't hear you."

I quickly glanced at my friends. I didn't want them to hear me, and thankfully, they weren't all staring at me, waiting for me to answer. "Water," I said a little louder.

"Water?" Casey shouted.

I sighed as all four sets of eyes turned to me. "Yes."

"And what else?"

"That's it."

"Okay. It's your birthday." Casey turned and headed for the bar.

April tilted her head. "I thought you were staying at Griffin's tonight?"

"That's what I planned," I said, playing with my purse zipper. It wasn't a lie. It was what I originally was going to do.

"Then, why are you drinking water?"

"And you gave me half your beer at the last place," Troy chimed in.

I lifted my hands in surrender. "I simply need to hydrate a little. I'm thirty now. I don't recover from hangovers like I did when I was twenty."

JJ frowned in confusion. "Don't you mean twenty-one?"

"Yeah, that too."

"Well, don't drink water for too long, or you're going to lose your buzz," Christina said.

That's the goal.

I gave her a thumbs-up.

"How's the wedding planning going?" I asked to change the subject. "As a bridesmaid, I keep waiting for you to call me up to do stuff."

"Ooh, yeah, fill us in," April added.

"My sister…" Christina looked up at the ceiling and back to her. "I love her. I really do. And most days, I'm thankful she offered to plan the wedding." She put her hands out and cupped them until they created a circle. "But sometimes, I want to strangle her." She started shaking her hands as she clenched her jaw.

I bit my lip as I tried not to laugh. "That bad, huh?"

Christina sagged as she dropped her arms. "I said no chocolate cake because Troy's mom is allergic. That's it. No chocolate. We could have any other kind, but it's like chocolate was the only option once I said it was a no go."

"Sorry, babe," I said.

She sighed. "It's fine. Sometimes, I just have to put my foot down."

At that moment, Casey brought our drinks over and handed them out. I picked up my water and swallowed a couple of big sips.

After Casey left, Christina started telling April a few other things about her wedding that I had already heard about. While April wasn't in the wedding, she had been invited and seemed very interested in what Christina had to say. Maybe she was going to plan her own wedding soon.

I was sitting, relaxed, enjoying the moment, when two drinks were plopped down in front of me.

I looked up to see Griffin standing there.

"Scoot," he told me.

Why can't he sit on the other end?

I didn't voice my question out loud because everyone at the table would notice, and despite my staring at him for several seconds and not moving, Griffin didn't budge.

I rolled my eyes and moved over but barely far enough for him to fit his whole ass on the seat.

He didn't seem to care because he sat so close that we were touching from shoulder to leg. My little plan had backfired, and now, if I moved, he would know I was trying to get away from him.

"Everything okay behind the bar?" I asked him.

"Yep." He moved the one drink closer to me. "Casey said you didn't order anything because you were worried about getting too drunk, so I brought you this. It doesn't have much alcohol, but it's more fun than water."

I couldn't turn down his gift when he had gone out of his way to think of me. And it was sweet of him.

I picked up my glass and sniffed what was inside. It smelled sweet. I probably didn't need the sugar any more than I needed alcohol, but I couldn't resist giving it a try.

"Mmm," I said and licked my lips. "It tastes good."

"Jesus," Griffin said again, and I stiffened. It was the same curse word he'd used when I asked him to sleep with me. But he didn't say any more.

He took a drink from his own glass. I was so busy watching that I wasn't prepared for his hand that was closest to me to land on my knee.

I froze.

Curiosity piqued, I wanted to know what he was doing and what he was going to do next.

He rubbed his thumb over my knee until I started to relax.

But even though I was no longer stiff, I didn't move.

Griffin ran his fingers up the inside of my leg until he hit my skirt, and then he went back down. He did this several times until I was squirming.

I was getting turned on. My breathing had picked up, and I was wet between my legs.

I had no idea what Griffin's goal was, but mine was to go home and break out my vibrator.

I should really stop drinking this time.

But when I looked at my glass, it was empty.

I hadn't even realized I was still drinking it.

Griffin raised his arm and used his finger to make a small circle, as if he was telling someone something about the whole table.

"What are you doing?" I hissed in his ear.

"Ordering us another round of drinks."

I leaned in closer, although I didn't have to go far since I was already sitting so close. "That's not what I meant, and you know it."

His hand disappeared from my leg.

Wait. I take it back. Forget I questioned you.

But he wasn't leaving. He put the hand that had been on my leg behind my head on the back of the booth. Shifting slightly toward me, he picked up my calf and pulled my leg over his.

I quickly looked at our friends to see if they were staring at us, but they weren't. And I really shouldn't be surprised. Griffin and I were close. His arm around me wasn't anything unusual.

No, what was unusual was his other palm sliding up my lower limb. And this time, he didn't stop at my skirt.

My eyes widened, but I quickly schooled my face before anyone asked questions.

However, I couldn't stop the little squeak that came out of me when his fingertips brushed my panties.

Holy shit. My best friend almost touched my vagina.

Almost became absolute when he drew my underwear aside and ran a finger up my slit.

I sucked in a breath and shivered.

With the hand behind my shoulder, Griffin nudged my head closer until his mouth was next to my ear.

"Damn, babe, you are soaked." He pushed two fingers into me and sucked in a breath. "Is this for me?"

I shook my head, and he started to pull his hand away.

I clamped my upper legs closed as much as I could with one still hanging on his lap.

I turned my head slightly toward him and whispered, "I lied. It's for you."

For telling the truth, I got a thumb on my clit.

I moaned softly.

"Do you like that?" Griffin's mouth was still next to my ear.

I squeezed my inner muscles around him.

He chuckled. "I can't wait for you to do that on my cock."

I slammed my hand down on his thigh and dug in my nails as he continued to work me under the table.

I hadn't had an orgasm in a long time, so I was embarrassingly close. But I couldn't come in front of all my friends. *Could I?*

"Why are you doing this?" I managed to whisper. Not only was I curious, but I was also hoping to distract my body from exploding at the slightest touch.

"This is what you wanted. What you asked me for."

"But you said no."

Griffin nipped my ear. "I did no such thing."

I replayed the scene in my head. He wasn't wrong. He hadn't actually told me no.

"It was implied," I said.

He nipped me again. "Stop thinking. This will be the orgasm that's so good that you don't care where you are." He repeatedly tapped his thumb against my clit, and I knew there was no more holding back. "Come now, Madeline. I've got you."

I let my head fall back against his shoulder and momentarily forgot about my friends, the other customers, and the fact that we were sitting in Griffin's bar.

My orgasm started between my legs and fanned out until it reached the top of my head and the tips of my toes. It tingled all over and felt like a white-hot heat passing through me.

God, it felt incredible.

I had indeed not cared where I was because all of a sudden, I heard voices and music again.

"Is Madeline okay?"

I didn't even bother lifting my head.

"I think she's tired," Griffin said, his fingers still inside me.

He slowly withdrew them, and I immediately felt empty.

Taking a deep breath, I looked up at my friends. "Griff's right. I'm spent, and I think I need to call it a night."

My best friend chuckled beside me and pulled his hand out from under my skirt.

At that moment, Mitch came over with another round of drinks.

After he set them on the table, I looked at Griffin. "I'm done drinking. I'd rather go upstairs and go to bed."

The corner of his mouth turned up. "As long as you understand that you won't be sleeping. We still have that leg-shaking orgasm we need to work on," he said, his words only for me.

NINE

GRIFFIN

I GENTLY TOOK Madeline's leg off mine and exited the booth.

"Feel free to finish my beer," I told Troy, Christina, April, and JJ. "I'm going to take the birthday girl upstairs and put her to bed."

"That's so cute. Are you going to tuck her in too?" Christina asked.

"Something like that," I muttered.

Madeline kicked me in the leg. "You can drink mine too," she said as she stood.

The two of us said good-bye to our friends and headed for the back stairs up to my apartment.

As soon as the bottom door was closed, I grabbed her hand and started pulling her up behind me.

She laughed. "Wow. Someone seems awfully excited."

I didn't comment because I thought she already knew the answer.

When Madeline had told me what she wanted me to

give her for her birthday earlier tonight, my sexual arousal had gone from zero to sixty in two seconds. My dick got so hard, I had to step away from her.

Honestly, I was a little afraid that I might say, *Fuck it*, to the crowded bar and take her right then and there.

Thankfully, I pulled myself together at the last second and concluded that maybe that particular moment was not the right one to give Madeline her birthday present.

The bad part was, she thought I had rejected her. I hadn't. I'd just needed to process the whole thing. I mean, the two of us in all our years as friends had never even kissed.

Speaking of which...

We reached my apartment door, so I tugged her close and pushed her up against the wall.

Her breath caught, and her brown eyes widened. "What are you doing?"

"I realized I still haven't kissed you." I cupped both her cheeks as I leaned down and slanted my mouth over hers.

Without any hesitation, she opened for me, and it was Madeline who wrapped her tongue around mine first as she fisted my shirt.

Being best friends, the two of us had discussed our sex lives quite regularly, so I knew she wasn't shy in bed and that she liked to fuck. But to actually experience her openness and eagerness in action was a whole other animal.

I still had the residual feeling of her contracting around my fingers downstairs in the booth. I wasn't going to forget that for as long as I lived.

The fact that I had given my best friend an orgasm in

front of everyone like that seemed surreal. I hadn't actually intended to take it that far.

Since she had refused to talk to me so I could explain I had only been shocked but that I was ready and willing to fulfill her desire, I'd decided to show her. But then she'd been so hot and wet, I hadn't been able to resist getting a better feel.

And now, I couldn't wait to get inside her.

I reached into my jeans pocket and pulled out my keys. Unfortunately, I had to pull my lips away from Madeline's to slide the key into the dead bolt.

She kissed my neck and licked my skin, and I pushed my door open so hard, it slammed against the wall.

I guided her inside and kicked the door with my foot. My bedroom seemed a million feet away, so I picked up Madeline and set her on the table I kept next to the front door for keys, mail, and apparently fucking my best friend.

Madeline pushed my shirt up my abdomen, so I reached behind me and pulled it over my head. I eased her legs apart and pressed myself between them.

As I took her mouth again, I pushed her skirt up and over her hips. I rubbed my hardness along her cleft and grinned when she moaned.

Reluctantly, I stepped back in order to remove her underwear. But it was worth it when the small scrap of fabric was lying on my floor. It also helped that Madeline unzipped my pants and pulled my cock out of my boxers.

I already knew what I was going to find when I put my hand between her legs, but the feel of her silken heat was still exciting and such a damn turn-on. I put my other hand over her throat because I wanted to feel her moan this time.

I was rewarded with the sound as soon as I flicked her clit.

Madeline wrapped her legs around the back of mine and pulled me closer. I moved my hands away, and my dick hit her bare pussy.

"Fuck," I said because I wanted to push inside more than I'd ever wanted with anyone else before.

It didn't help that my little minx of a best friend began rotating her hips as she used my erection for her pleasure.

I almost stood there and watched her, but I was too selfish. I wanted to be deep inside her when her next orgasm hit.

I pulled open the drawer under and off to the side of us. Another thing I used the table for was condoms because I never knew when I was going to need protection.

Like right now.

I quickly tore open the wrapper, but Madeline snatched the latex out of my hands before I could pull it out.

I threw the wrapper aside and stared as she rolled it down my cock. She barely finished covering me when I kissed her and drove inside her.

Madeline's head fell back as I pumped my hips. Her nails dug into my back, and little cries and moans were coming from the back of her throat. I didn't think I had ever heard anything as sexy as that in my life.

I pressed my lips to her throat and sucked on the spot between there and her shoulder. Her pussy tightened around me, so I did it again.

But I wanted more.

I yanked her so far to the edge that she would have fallen off if I wasn't holding her up. This time, instead of sucking, I bit down on her neck as I shoved my cock in as deep as I could go.

Her pussy contracted around my shaft, and her legs began to shake as she let go of me and lost her balance. I held on tight as her orgasm swept through her body, fearing she might actually fall off the table.

But once I was sure she had regained some control over her muscles, I began to thrust again. Her inner muscles were still squeezing me, and as much as I wanted to work her for another orgasm, it wasn't going to happen.

Madeline felt too good.

Still, as I focused more on my own pleasure than hers now, I noticed that her breathing had quickened again.

I smiled next to her ear and threaded my fingers through her hair. "Are you going to come again?"

"No," she said right before she cried out and fell back against my arm.

And like that, I was done for. I had to catch myself with my free hand on the table before I landed on top of Madeline; my orgasm was so strong.

I came in a hot rush, and white lights filled my vision. I was sure I had blown the end of the condom; I came so hard.

I had no idea how long I had been standing there, waiting for my senses to return to normal, but it couldn't have been too long because when I stood up straight, Madeline's eyes were closed, and she had a small smile on her face.

I brushed my thumb over her lips. "You okay?"

"Mmhmm."

I kissed her temple. "So, leg-shaking orgasm. Check. Now that round one is complete, are you ready for round two?"

Her eyes opened, and she blinked at me. "Round two?"

"Yeah, babe. After all, your birthday isn't over yet."

TEN

MADELINE

MY PHONE WENT OFF next to my head. It was my Taylor Swift ringtone reserved only for my mom.

I cracked my eyes open just enough to find my phone and answer it. "Hello?"

"Happy birthday!"

"Thank you." My voice sounded like I had smoked a pack of cigarettes last night.

"Madeline, are you sleeping?"

"I was."

"I'm sorry. It's almost ten, so I figured you'd be awake."

"It's okay. I should get up anyway."

"I forgot you went out last night with your friends. Did you have fun? Did you stay up late?"

The night before ran through my head, and I gasped.

"What's wrong?" my mother asked.

"Nothing. Just a headache."

There was no way I could tell her I was having déjà vu because this was how I'd woken up on Wednesday. Only this time, I was naked and tender between my legs from all the times we'd screwed the night before. I hadn't had that much sex since college.

I bit my lip and whimpered in regret as I slowly turned over to look at Griffin. I wasn't ready to face him, but it was pretty hard to avoid it when I was in his bed.

Last night, asking my best friend to have sex with me had seemed like an excellent idea. But I hadn't considered how awkward I would feel the morning after. To make matters worse, I couldn't claim I had blacked out from drinking. No, I remembered every naughty detail. And I had no idea what I was going to say to him.

A big sigh of relief escaped me when I saw him lying on his stomach, a pillow pulled over his head and his breathing deep and even.

"Honey, are you sure you're okay?"

Not now, Mom.

I rolled away. "Can I call you back?" I asked softly.

"Why are you whispering? I can barely hear you."

"Mom, I have to go," I said instead of answering her. I didn't care if she knew I'd slept at Griffin's because she knew we had done it before. But I did care if my voice woke up Griffin.

I closed my eyes and buried my face in the pillow.

I couldn't believe I had slept with my best friend.

I needed time to process this. Preferably at home and far away from Griffin.

"Madeline? Are you still there?"

And not when I was on the phone with my mother.

"I'll call you back," I said and hung up. I quickly turned my ringer to silent before she called me again.

63

I ordered my brain to focus, so I could concoct a plan of action.

I needed to sneak out of bed, get dressed, and leave, all without waking up Griffin.

The bed moved under me, and I knew it was too late.

I heard him and felt him move quite a bit. I willed my body to relax, so hopefully, he'd think I was asleep.

"Is your mom going to wake you up every morning you stay at my place?" he asked, snaking an arm around my waist. "It's becoming a tradition."

"Uh…" I couldn't form a coherent answer when I felt Griffin's hardness hit my bare butt.

I closed my eyes as I remembered pushing his pants down his hips and seeing his dick for the first time. I'd never thought he was small. He was too tall and muscular.

But I hadn't expected his cock to be so huge either. The outline in his underwear hadn't done him justice.

I had gotten so excited, I'd stolen the condom out of his hand, so I could be the one to put it on. I had wanted to touch it. I'd wanted to touch him.

My eyes flew open as Griffin pulled my leg up and over his hip. He put a hand between my legs and groaned behind me.

"Mads, you're already wet. What are you thinking about?"

"I plead the Fifth," I said.

He chuckled, and his hand disappeared. I briefly felt his body pull away from mine as he did something behind me.

I didn't realize what he was doing until his chest was flush against me once more and he was sliding into me. I didn't know why it hadn't occurred to me that he could be getting another condom.

I shivered and squirmed on his thickness. "Holy shit," I murmured.

Griffin's big hand ran up my belly, and he cupped my breast and flicked my nipple. "Sorry, I forgot to warn you. I like morning sex."

I didn't get a chance to respond because he started thrusting inside of me.

And just like that, I went from wanting to sneak out to letting him take complete control of my body.

If I was lucky, he'd fall back asleep in post-coital bliss, and then I could leave. But until then, I might as well enjoy how good he made me feel because I already knew another orgasm was barreling toward me.

Griffin wasn't the only one who liked morning sex.

My plan had worked well, except that I had fallen asleep too. I woke up forty-five minutes later and carefully snuck out of Griffin's bed. After grabbing my clothes from his bedroom floor, I tiptoed out of the bedroom before getting dressed.

I was so worried that he'd wake up that I left the apartment without using the bathroom. Thankfully, the bar hadn't opened yet, so I quickly used the restroom down there.

As I walked out, my stomach growled.

I hadn't slept in this late in a long time. My body didn't

know what to do without its usual breakfast and morning coffee.

I swung by a drive-through that served all-day breakfast and ordered extra coffee. By the time I ate my food, drank my java, got home, and showered, I felt a little more like myself.

While I had scrubbed my back, I'd thought about what to do about the sleeping-with-Griffin situation, and I'd concluded the smartest thing to do was to pretend like last night—and this morning—never happened.

I usually wasn't shy about sex, but even the thought of talking to my best friend about what we had done made my face heat. I had no idea what had gotten into me.

And that was why it was best to act like nothing unusual had happened.

Telling myself what I was going to do was one thing. Acting on it was another.

Ten minutes after I showered, Griffin called. And rather than answering like I would normally do, I ignored it.

He was going to think I was such a chicken.

"*Bwak, bwak,*" I said to myself.

ELEVEN

GRIFFIN

MY PHONE RANG, and I did my last rep before setting my barbell down.

I thought that maybe Madeline was finally calling me back, but it was her mom.

"Hello?"

"Hello, Griffin."

"Hi, Nora. It's not every day I get a phone call from you."

"Have you talked to Madeline? I thought she said she was staying at your place last night, so she wouldn't have to drive home. Did you see her this morning? I talked to her for a few minutes, but she said we'd talk later. And now, she's not answering her phone."

I chuckled. "She's not answering for me either."

"Well, that girl…" Nora said with exasperation.

"But, yes, she did stay last night. I did see her briefly, but then I fell back asleep. She left while I was out." *Simply left? Or did she sneak out?*

"You are such a nice boy to let my daughter sleep on your couch."

I cleared my throat. "Yeah, that's me."

"I suppose you're no longer a boy, are you? To me, part of you will always be the kid who came over to my house and snuck food out of my cupboards."

I laughed. "You always had the good stuff my mom wouldn't buy."

"Since we're talking about you eating my food, how would you like to come to dinner tomorrow night? We're doing a small family celebration for Madeline's birthday. It will just be Madeline, her dad, me, and my mother is coming."

"I'd love to come."

While George Campbell wasn't a second dad like his wife was a second mom, I had always gotten along with him. He was more serious and reserved than Nora. But he was still the one who had helped me when I fell off my bike in elementary school. He had taken me into the house and cleaned up my knee and elbow with barely a word.

Madeline's grandma, Dotty, however, was fun. She was loud and told it like it was. She always made me laugh.

Plus, I had a feeling that Madeline was avoiding me. I would give her today and tomorrow to realize that the two of us sleeping together wasn't going to affect our friendship. But she couldn't avoid me forever. Dinner with her family was perfect. They would give us a buffer, so she could see that our friendship hadn't changed.

"Wonderful," Nora said. "Since my daughter is ignoring her mother, how would you like to decide what kind of cake I should make?"

"My favorite is yellow cake with chocolate frosting."

"That's right. I helped Madeline make you a cake for your birthday one year."

That had to have been back in high school. Maybe even middle school.

"Chocolate frosting on yellow cake it is."

"Don't forget to add thirty candles."

Nora laughed. "I think the smoke detectors might go off if I did that."

"You're probably right. It would be fun to see her face though."

"I'll see what I can do," she said in that mom tone of voice that told me she would do everything she could to put thirty candles on Madeline's birthday cake.

My phone beeped in my ear.

"Can you hold on a second?" I asked.

"Yes."

I looked to see who had texted me. It was the birthday girl.

> Madeline: Sorry. I was in the shower when you called, and now, I'm heading into the grocery store. Why did you call? Did you need something?

I put my phone back to my ear. "Madeline just sent me a text."

Nora scoffed. "Well, now, she's definitely getting all thirty candles on her cake."

I laughed. "I'm sure she'll call you back soon. She said she was going into a store."

"She'd better." She sighed. "I will see you tomorrow evening then?"

"Yep. What time should I be there?"

"Can you be here by six?"

"I sure can." I could go over to my parents' to visit before I went to the Campbells' for dinner. I had better warn my mom I wasn't eating there though.

"Have a good rest of the weekend, Griffin."

"Thank you. You too."

I hung up with Nora and pulled up my text messages.

> Me: No. Nothing important. You left while I was sleeping, and I only wanted to make sure you were okay.

> Madeline: Sorry about that.

> Me: You weren't sneaking out, were you?

I wasn't going to beat around the bush when it came to my best friend.

> Madeline: No!

> Me: Okay, because you know that you don't have to avoid me, right?

> Madeline: I know that.

> Me: Just checking.

> Madeline: I have a few more errands to run, and then I'll call you later. Sound good? Or did you have plans?

She wished.

> Me: Work, but I should be able to answer my phone.

> Madeline: Okay.

> Me: Are you still planning to come by the bar later now that dinner with Harris was canceled?

> Madeline: Sure.

I'd believe that when I saw it.

> Me: Okay. Talk later then?

> Madeline: Later.

I finished my workout, showered, and made my way downstairs. One of my bartenders had already opened for me, and while it was busier than a weekday afternoon, the small crowd was nothing compared to weekend nights.

I waved hello and said, "Come get me if you need any help."

The bartender nodded, and I went to my office.

I'd had no idea owning a bar would involve so much paperwork, but it was still worth it and made me appreciate my finance and business degree. I had always known I wanted to start my own place and almost skipped out of going to college. But after some serious discussions with Madeline, I'd decided to go.

Sure, my student loans were a pain to pay every month, but I wouldn't have been ready to open a business at eighteen, and admittedly, I'd learned more at my six-month internship than I did in class. In the end, it was worth it.

I spent the afternoon in my office and left when I heard the noise picking up outside my door.

It wasn't until I crawled into bed at three in the morning that I realized Madeline had never called me or stopped by.

She was definitely avoiding me.

TWELVE
MADELINE

SUNDAY NIGHT, I was running late to my birthday dinner with my parents. At the last minute, my mom had called and asked me to pick up rolls. I'd told her they weren't needed, but she'd claimed that my father would complain if he didn't have them.

As I pulled up a little after six, I saw Griffin's car in front of his parents' house next door. I almost hit the gas and sped off, but I told myself I was being ridiculous. Griffin was my best friend. So what if we'd had sex? It wasn't like the world was coming to an end. I just needed to face him again and get it over with to show myself that everything was normal.

Not tonight though. I had dinner plans that I was overdue for.

Or so I told myself.

Realizing that I was being a chicken, I decided I would go to My Favorite Place tomorrow after work.

Feeling good about my plan of action, I parked, got out of my car, and walked into my parents' house. The first person I saw was my grandma Dotty.

"Happy birthday," she said as she held her arms out for a hug.

"Hi, Grandma." I squeezed her tight.

She smelled like her favorite Chanel No. 5 perfume, like always.

"It's been too long, kid."

I released her and stepped back. "I know. I'm a horrible granddaughter."

"Not horrible, but you could do better."

I laughed. She didn't pull any punches, my grandmother.

I looked around. "Where is everyone?" I held up the grocery bag. "I brought the rolls my mother insisted that she needed."

"Your father's in the living room, watching football, and your mother's in the kitchen."

My parents' house was old, and the front door opened to an entryway with the stairs to the top floor straight ahead. To the right was basically the rest of the house. A living room, dining room, and kitchen from front to back. Open concept it was not, but they had lived here my whole life and weren't going anywhere soon.

My grandma and I headed into the living room, where I saw my father in his favorite chair, watching the football game.

"Hey, Dad."

He glanced at me for a second. "Hi, peanut." His attention was already back on the TV.

"What kind of beer do you want?" a muffled but deep voice called from the kitchen.

My father yelled back, "Miller Lite."

I wrinkled my nose in confusion. "Who's here?" It'd almost sounded like—

"One Miller Lite com—" Griffin grinned when he saw me. "Hey, Mads. You're here."

My eyes widened, and my heart sped up. "Griffin. What are you doing here?"

"Your mom invited me," he said as he walked toward me. He handed my dad a beer and then sat on the couch, opening his own bottle.

"When did you talk to my mom?"

"Saturday," he said, eyes on the television. "You'd know that if I saw you last night."

He was totally calling me on my shit.

"Sorry. I ended up treating myself to takeout and a movie, and I fell asleep early."

A brow went up.

"I swear." I chuckled. "I guess I'm getting old now that I'm thirty." Plus, someone had kept me up most of the night before that. I had been truly tired last night.

"Sorry you were all alone."

"I was fine. Really. If I had been lonely, I would have stopped by the bar."

Liar, liar, pants on fire.

He seemed to accept my response because he nodded and jerked his head toward the kitchen. "You'd better get those rolls in the kitchen. Your mom is starting to panic."

"Will do."

I spun slowly on my heel as I took in the first conversation Griffin and I'd had after we had lots and lots of sex.

It was like nothing had changed. I didn't know what I'd expected from him. Some sort of sexual innuendo or knowing glances, I supposed. But everything was the same as usual. He was the same Griffin as always.

And as I headed in the direction of the kitchen, I felt foolish for freaking out about seeing my best friend again.

"When are you going to hit that, Madeline?" Grandma Dotty asked.

I stopped in my tracks. "*Oh my God*," I said in shock.

"If I were ten years younger, I'd be all over that boy like white on rice. He's so polite and good-looking. Tall too." She wiggled her eyebrows. "I bet he's—"

"*Grandma. Jeez.*"

She shrugged. "I'm only stating facts, kid. You'd better snatch that hunk up before someone else does."

Someone, please rescue me from this conversation.

My mom poked her head out of the kitchen, and she smiled when she saw me. "You're here."

I quickly ran to her and handed her the buns with a sigh of relief.

"What's wrong?" she asked, her face full of alarm now.

"Your mother is a dirty old woman."

Mom laughed. "What else is new? Last time you visited, she told you about three dates she had been on in one week."

My grandfather had passed away ten years ago, and my grandmother was determined to find husband number two.

"She told me that if she were ten years younger, she'd be on Griffin like white on rice," I whispered. "Never mind that I don't ever want to picture that in my head, but she'd still be twenty years older than him."

My mom laughed. "I don't think that's stopped your grandmother in the past."

"Gross."

Grandma walked into the kitchen. "What did I miss?"

"Nothing," I said quickly.

"Madeline's worried you're moving in on her man," Mom said.

I rolled my eyes and shook my head. "He's not my man."

Grandma patted my arm. "Don't worry, kid. He's safe from me. He only has eyes for you."

I didn't think he had eyes for me so much as he didn't have eyes for anyone else in this house. Besides, I was the best friend. It was obvious he would look at me the most.

"I think he's just not ready to date you yet, Grandma."

She laughed. "Whatever you say, kid."

After my mother maintained that I wasn't allowed to help her cook since it was my birthday dinner, she pushed me out of the kitchen, and I had nowhere else to go, except to sit down next to Griffin.

I couldn't help the flutter of nerves in my stomach, even after he had greeted me like usual, but I didn't need to worry because neither he nor my father looked my way as I sat down on the couch.

I tried to watch the game, but I wasn't into football, and my eyes wandered to my best friend.

He was leaning forward, his elbows on his knees, obviously into the game. His large hands were wrapped around his beer bottle. I never really thought hands were that sexy before, but the memories of those hands touching me all over was making me hot.

Literally and figuratively.

I felt like someone had turned up the thermostat, and my nipples were hard while I got a tingle between my legs.

I was just about to get up and insist my mom give me a job to do when Griffin swung his beer bottle away from him and over to me. He was still staring at the screen.

"What are you doing?" I asked.

"You keep staring at my beer. I figured you wanted some since you hadn't grabbed one for yourself."

I chuckled. *No, I don't want your beer. I want you.*

But I couldn't tell him that.

Instead, I took the bottle from him and downed a couple of sips before running the cold bottle over my forehead.

"Dinner's ready," my mom yelled from the kitchen.

"Great," I said and pushed the bottle back to Griffin.

His fingers brushed mine as he took his beer.

I whimpered as I jumped up from my seat.

"You okay?" he asked.

"Just hungry." I turned and headed for the table before he could tell I was lying.

THIRTEEN
MADELINE

MY PARENTS' home only had two bathrooms, and since my father was occupying the main-floor one, I headed upstairs.

I didn't make it to the top floor much anymore since I'd moved out because there really was no reason to, so walking up the steps flooded me with memories of growing up there.

After using the bathroom, I continued my journey to my old bedroom. It was still the same as when I had gone to college over a decade ago. My mom had said she didn't need to use it for anything—they already had a guest room —so she left it as it was.

I thumbed a couple of participation awards I had hung on the wall and a couple of old notebooks I had left on my desk. I sat down on my double bed, and I turned on the bedside lamp since the light over the stairs didn't quite reach this far into my room.

On the bottom shelf of my nightstand were some photo albums. I had forgotten they were there.

I pulled out the thickest one and slowly opened it.

I loved photo albums. They were work, but they had a magical quality that scrolling through one's phone lacked.

The photos started when I had been in middle school, but as I flipped through the pages, I also came upon high school pictures. I smiled at the image of me and Griffin on our first day as freshmen. I remembered being so nervous, worried I was going to get picked on or hazed, but Griffin stood with his arms crossed, casually leaning against the tree we were posing in front of.

He had grown several inches the last few months of middle school and the summer after. His shoulders had broadened, and he had put on muscle. It wasn't any wonder he hadn't been worried. He'd looked like he was at least a junior.

"What are you looking at?"

I lifted my head to see Griffin standing in the doorway. "High school pics."

He walked over and flopped down onto the bed behind me. "I was worried you hadn't come back because you were mad."

I spun my head to look over my shoulder and frowned. "Why would I be mad?"

"Because your mom put so many candles on your cake at my suggestion."

I had found it odd that my mother had insisted we all go outside for me to blow out the candles on my birthday cake even if it was a relatively warm and peaceful fall night. When I had seen the two number candles that spelled out thirty with thirty candles surrounding them, I'd understood why.

I turned my head back around and chuckled. "No, I'm

not mad. You might be trying to make me feel old, but I'm still the youngest in the house, so the joke's on all of you."

"Touché." Griffin put his hand on my side and squeezed. "I want to see too."

Enjoying his touch too much, I pivoted ninety degrees and leaned up against the headboard.

When I had gotten my double-size bed, I remembered thinking it was so big compared to my twin. But seeing Griffin lying on it next to me, it was apparent that it was too small. Or maybe he was just that large.

Griffin rolled toward me and leaned against my side.

It wasn't an unusual move and one I wouldn't normally blink at, but after Friday night, I was much more aware of the big, handsome man beside me.

He didn't seem to be fazed by me at all though.

He laughed and pointed to a picture. "What were we doing?"

It was a photo of the two of us with a group of friends at school, but we were all wearing what looked like pajamas.

"Homecoming week, I think. PJ Day."

"That's right." He looked up at me. "Cute bunnies."

"Hey, bunnies were all the rage back then." I tapped my finger over him on the photo. "And it's certainly better than your football jersey and sweatpants. You can't tell me that's what you wore to bed." Jerseys were made of mesh and not something I would want to sleep in.

He lifted a shoulder. "It wasn't. But I couldn't wear just my boxers to school. I would have gotten in trouble."

"Okay, that makes sense."

And now, I was picturing Griffin only wearing his boxers. Griffin now, not high school Griffin.

I swallowed and turned the page, hoping to distract myself from thoughts of my best friend almost naked.

Or him naked and lying over me, moving inside of—

Griffin snapped his fingers in front of my face. "Earth to Madeline." His brows lifted. "You okay? You look…" He tilted his head to get a better view of me, but I couldn't let him guess what I had been thinking about.

"I'm fine. Thinking about high school, is all." I flipped a page. "Part of me feels like it was so long ago, and another part feels like it was yesterday."

Despite my wayward sexual thoughts, this was true. I couldn't believe how much time had passed.

"It does. I'm glad I'm not back there though."

"Really? But you had so much fun. And you were a jock." Which meant he had gotten away with a lot with the teachers and he'd had his share of female attention.

"Yeah, it was fun, but I like my life now."

"That's good, I suppose. There's no going back."

I continued to flip through the pages, the two of us pausing to look and comment on pictures every now and then. I was starting to loosen up and realize that no matter what, Griffin was still my best friend, and nothing was going to change that.

We were getting to the end of the album, where we were dressed up in formal clothes.

"Is this prom?"

"No. This is still sophomore year. It can't be prom yet."

"Then, why are we so dressed up?"

I flipped a page, and once I saw Griffin's date, I knew when it was.

"Ugh. It was Spring Fling. The dance where the girl was

supposed to ask the guy. You know, because we lived in the 1800s, and women weren't allowed to make the first move, except for the special dance where we were given permission," I added sarcastically.

Griffin chuckled. "Oh yeah. I remember. Jeanene Hanson asked me to go. You know, she was a senior, and I was only—"

"A sophomore. Yes, I know." I rolled my eyes.

"You're just jealous because you went with Billy Richardson, who was a sophomore."

"I liked Billy Richardson. Remember, I was the one who asked him to go. Besides, why would I be jealous of your lack of taste?"

"Ooh, them's fightin' words, Campbell."

"Well...I mean...Jeanene did get kicked out of high school and had her daddy buy her way back in."

"She was suspended."

I snorted. "Sure, that was the line they were feeding everyone, but we all know she got booted out. It must be nice to have rich parents to throw money at your problems." I looked down at Griffin. "You realize she probably asked you because none of the seniors or juniors would go with her."

He shrugged. "I didn't care back then. She gave me head behind the bleachers on the football field. That's all that mattered to me."

"You're gross." I quickly turned the last two pages and lifted my arm to nudge Griffin off me. "That's it."

I would like to think I was pushing him away because we were done with the album, but I was irritated with myself for being bothered by Griffin getting a blow job from Jeanene Hanson all those years ago.

I leaned over and slid the picture album back in its place on my nightstand. "Should we look at more?" I asked in an attempt to get in a better mood.

Griffin wrapped his arm around my waist and pulled me back toward him. "How about you just lie here with me?"

I wanted to refuse because I was annoyed with him, but he was solid and warm, and he smelled good. "Okay. Ten minutes."

"Ten minutes," he agreed, and his breathing soon evened out.

I closed my eyes and started counting to thirty as I slowed my breathing and cleared my thoughts.

I didn't even remember making it to twenty.

FOURTEEN
GRIFFIN

I OPENED my eyes to unfamiliar surroundings. It took my vision a second to adjust to see that I was in Madeline's old room in her parents' house. She was snuggled up against me with her breath tickling my neck, and the lamp beside the bed was off.

Either she had turned it off or someone else had come in here and done it.

I looked at my watch. It was only a little after eight, and I had been sleeping less than an hour.

I gently shook Madeline. "Mads."

She threw a leg over me, and I smiled.

I shook her again. "Mads. It's time to get up."

She groaned and rolled onto her back. "What time is it?"

"Eight."

"That's it?"

"I know. It feels like midnight now that the sun goes down so early."

She got onto her elbows. "I can't believe I fell asleep."

"Why? I'm cuddly like a bunny."

She snorted at my reference to her high school pajamas. "You're cuddly like a rock," she said as she sat up and swung her legs to the floor.

"Like a rock?"

"All your muscles, they're hard."

I scoffed. I wasn't that muscular. Sure, I worked out, but I wasn't going to win any bodybuilding contests. Not that I wanted to. Sometimes, less was more.

"Yeah, well, you didn't seem to mind on Friday. What did you say to me again?" I paused for dramatic effect and snapped my fingers. "That's right. You told me you wanted to lick me all over."

Madeline jumped up from the bed and peeked over her shoulder at me. "It's not the same thing."

I sat up and tried to look at her face, but it was too dark. The only light coming into the room was from the stairs.

"Are you embarrassed?"

"No," she said too quickly as she yanked on the hem of her shirt.

I threw my head back and laughed. "You totally are."

I snagged her hand and pulled her back down to the bed. She yelped as she fell into my arms.

I ran my nose along her jaw. "It's okay to think I'm sexy, Mads. Most women do."

She slapped her hands down on my shoulders. "That's what you think."

"Hmm," I murmured and trailed my mouth down to the spot between her shoulder and her neck.

I brushed my lips over her skin, and she drew in a breath.

I licked her once and then quickly sucked on her there.

God, she tastes good.

Friday night memories came to the forefront of my brain, and I began to grow hard against her leg.

But if she knew I was turned on, it would defeat the purpose of my little move.

Madeline dug her nails into my shoulders, and I lifted my head.

"See? Women want me." I slapped her ass and jumped off the bed. Discreetly, I adjusted my dick in my jeans.

"You're the worst," she said and rolled off the bed.

Sighing dramatically, I put my hands on my hips. "Again, you told me I was the best on Friday. Why do you keep lying?" I bit my lip to keep from smiling.

"I did not say you were the best."

"That's right. I think it went something like, 'So good, so good, soooo—'"

She socked me in the gut. "I'm going downstairs," she muttered and left the room.

I sprinted after her and stopped her at the bottom of the stairs. "Hey, Mads."

She turned around. "What?"

I reached the same stair. I could hear the TV in the living room, so there was a strong chance that no one could hear us talking, but I leaned close and lowered my voice just in case. "I'm only teasing you, I hope you know. I'm not trying to upset you."

I leaned back, so I could see her eyes.

She smiled. "I know."

"Good." I put my mouth near her ear again. "Because you're beautiful, and the way you fuck..." I sucked in a breath through my teeth. "I'm surprised you don't have guys knocking down your door." I kissed her on the temple and continued down the stairs.

Madeline followed me into the living room, where her parents and grandmother were sitting around the television.

"Good morning, you two," Nora said jokingly.

"Sorry about falling asleep. I'm not a great dinner guest."

She waved her hand at me. "It's the weekend. Weekends are for naps. The two of you looked so peaceful, and I figured you needed your sleep."

"I was wondering who had turned the lamp off," Madeline said.

"Yeah, I lost quite a bit of sleep on Friday night for Madeline's birthday. She kept me up all night."

Nora looked at her daughter. "Madeline, I thought your partying days were over."

Madeline turned red and shot me a look. "Griff is exaggerating. But I did need sleep because you're right, Mom; my partying days are over."

"That's too bad," Grandma Dotty said. "I thought, with that bedhead, you two were doing something more fun than sleeping."

"Mom," Nora said.

"I'm out of here," George said and pushed himself off his recliner.

Madeline put her hand on his arm. "Have a good night, Dad."

He hugged her. "Good night, peanut. Happy birthday."

"Thanks."

"Are you really leaving?" her mom asked as George walked away.

"Yeah. I have to go to work tomorrow."

"Same for me," I said.

Nora frowned. "I understand." She stood and gave Madeline a hug. "Happy birthday."

"Thanks, Mom. Thanks for dinner and the birthday money."

"You're welcome."

As Madeline went to hug her grandma, Nora put her arms around me. "Thanks for coming, Griffin."

"My pleasure. You know I love your food."

She chuckled as she stepped away from me. "You know you're always welcome. With or without Madeline."

The two of us said good-bye, grabbed our stuff, and walked out the front door.

"Hey. Come over to my car real quick."

"Okay," Madeline said and walked over to my vehicle with me.

I unlocked the passenger door and pulled out a small present. "It's late, but here is your birthday present."

Her mouth popped open, and her eyes widened in surprise.

"You didn't think I forgot, did you?"

She took the box. "No…"

I laughed. "Making you come was not a birthday present, Mads. Even if it was something you'd asked me for." I nodded toward the gift. "Open it."

"Okay." She picked at a corner until she slowly pulled away the wrapping.

She was killing me with how slow she was going.

89

"Just rip it."

"It's too pretty."

I didn't understand women sometimes. It was wrapping paper that she was only going to throw away later.

Finally, she pulled all the wrapping away and opened the box.

She gasped.

FIFTEEN
MADELINE

I HAD no idea what Griffin had decided to get me since I'd never given him any ideas. And it turned out that he hadn't needed my help at all because he had just gifted me the best present I'd ever received.

"I can't believe you did this," I said.

"The way you say it, it sounds like I did a bad thing."

I shook my head. "No. You did a great thing. It's just that my gift sucks compared to yours," I said.

"Nah."

"Griffin, I got you a neon sign for your bar. You bought me two plane tickets to Europe."

He shrugged as if it were no big deal. "You always said you wanted to go before you turned thirty."

"That was years ago."

"I figured you gave it up after a while. But I thought if you couldn't go before you were thirty, why not go because you're thirty?"

I threw myself in his arms. "You're the best."

"Finally, you admit it."

I laughed into his chest. "Ha. You wish."

He rubbed my back. "So, does this mean you like your present?"

I stepped back. "Of course I like it, you big dummy."

He grinned. "Good. Now, no pressure, but if you really want to show me your thanks, you'll take me with you."

I laughed and slapped his arm with the tickets. "Duh. You're my best friend after all." I lifted my brow. "Besides, you already put your name on the other ticket."

He shrugged. "You never know. You might have a new boyfriend by then. I made sure the tickets are transferable."

I looked at the tickets again. They were for summer.

As if he'd read my mind, he said, "I guessed you wouldn't want to go in winter; plus, I wanted to give you time to take off work."

He was pretty thoughtful.

I looked back up to him. "I don't care if I have a new boyfriend." And I didn't really want a new boyfriend either. "I'm taking you with me."

He smiled. "Can't wait."

"Will you be able to leave your wife though?" I asked.

His brow furrowed. "My wife?"

"Yeah. You know, the bar. Are you sure you can leave her for a week?"

"You're so funny. Not."

I laughed.

"Yes, I can leave her. It's not every day that I get to go to Europe."

The front door to Griffin's parents' house opened.

"Happy birthday, Madeline," Griffin's mom, Camile, shouted.

92

"Thank you," I called back.

"Would you like to come in? I have something for you."

"I'd love to."

Camile turned her attention to her son. "You're coming in to say good-bye?"

"Yes," he shouted back. "You ready to go in there?" he asked me.

"Lead the way," I told him.

Camile gave me a hug as soon as I walked through the door. "Did you have a good birthday?"

"Yes. I had to work, but my coworkers brought treats. And we went out on Friday night. I even managed to get Griffin away from the bar for a while."

"You're a better woman than me. I can't get him to leave that place."

I put my hand up like I was telling Camile a secret, but I didn't bother to lower my voice. "I just told him the bar was his wife, but he didn't think I was funny."

Griffin put his hands on his hips. "I'm standing right here."

"Good," his mom said, "because that bar isn't going to give me grandchildren." She held up her hands. "Not that I'm asking for some right now. I'm only asking for some *someday*."

He sighed. "Where's Dad?"

"I'm right here," Glen, Griffin's father, said as he rounded the corner. His eyes brightened when he saw me. "Is that the birthday girl?"

I grinned. "Hi, Glen."

He came toward me and wrapped me in his arms. Glen was like an uncle to me. He was tall, like his son, but huskier.

When I was a kid, I'd always thought of him as a human teddy bear.

Pulling away, he asked, "What did my son get you? Something good, I hope."

I lifted the plane tickets and shook them as I did a little dance.

"Griffin, you bought those?" his mom asked, eyes wide.

I frowned. I hadn't expected disapproval from Camile.

Or maybe I was assuming things.

"Yes, Mom. It's not every day your best friend turns thirty."

"Well, I think it's an excellent present," Glen said. He squinted and leaned closer. "It also looks like you get something out of it, Griff." He chuckled. He put his hand on his wife's back. "It's a good gift, Cam."

"It's a lot of money."

The tension I hadn't known I'd even had in my shoulders lessened. She was just worried about her son spending a lot of money.

"The bar's had a good year, Mom."

Camile opened her mouth, but Griffin stopped her with a hand.

"I'm still putting plenty of money into savings."

Camile closed her lips and appeared to relax. "As long as you're not going to go broke, then I guess I can't complain."

"Did you give Madeline our present?" Glen asked Camile.

"I can't give it to her *now*. It pales in comparison."

"I will love it, no matter what it is."

"Famous last words," Camile said and headed to the

kitchen. A few seconds later, she came back with a gift bag. "Don't laugh."

"I would never," I promised.

I peeled back the tissue paper and pulled out an envelope and a handmade scarf. It was teal.

"Griffin said it was your favorite color."

"It is. It's beautiful."

Camile looked sheepish. "I figured, with winter coming, it never hurts to have an extra scarf."

I wrapped it around the back of my neck and threw one side over my shoulder. "Thank you. I love it."

"Don't forget the envelope."

I opened the white lid and pulled out a gift card to Caribou Coffee.

"We didn't know what else to get you, and Griffin said you liked coffee."

"I do." I looked up at both of them. "I love coffee. Thank you again. You didn't have to get me anything."

Glen shook his head at me and turned to Griffin. "Come with me to the garage. I forgot to show you something."

"I'll be right back," he told me.

"It's fine."

We'd driven separately after all. I didn't need him in order to leave.

Griffin and his dad walked into the kitchen and presumably out to the garage since I heard the door open and close.

"Glen got a new power tool. Those two were outside, looking at it, for an hour before he went to your parents' for dinner."

I smiled. Griffin and his dad were close, so this didn't surprise me. Both of his parents had been nervous about him opening a bar, but his father had been behind him one hundred percent and even offered to loan him money if he needed it.

"I have one more thing for you," Camile said as she turned and went toward the kitchen.

I followed her as she opened up a bakery tin and pulled out some cookies to put in a plastic food storage bag.

"I made your favorite cookies, so I thought you'd like to take some home."

"Chocolate chip?" I asked.

Camile made the best chocolate chip cookies. She'd given me the recipe, and I had attempted to make them a few times. They never tasted as good.

"You bet," she said.

While Camile put some cookies into a bag for me, I put my scarf, gift card, and plane tickets into the gift bag for safekeeping.

"I hope you're not mad that Griffin bought me those tickets. I want you to know I didn't ask for them. They were a total surprise."

Camile sealed the bag and handed it to me. "I'm not mad." She smiled reassuringly. "I just worry sometimes."

I tilted my head. "What do you mean?"

She sighed and looked reluctant to tell me. She stood up straight and said, "I love that Griffin has as good of a friend as you. I'm glad you have each other. I sometimes worry, is all. I worry that having you around prevents him from finding someone. Or if he does find someone, they'll never compare to you. I mean, how would a new girlfriend feel when she finds out that Griffin is going to Europe with another woman?"

I gave my response some thought before I said anything.

"I understand your fears. I would never stand in Griffin's way of being with someone. And you might not know it, but he does date. Many times, they don't get serious enough for him to introduce you to them."

"That's what worries me. What if he doesn't get serious because of you?"

I shook my head. "Trust me, he's always ended things for the right reasons. And until recently, I had my own boyfriend. I really don't think I'd stop Griffin from finding someone." I squeezed Camile's arm. "And if it helps, if he did find someone before the trip, I would pay him for his ticket and take someone else. Or maybe his new girlfriend could come with us." I swallowed, not liking the idea of Griffin with someone. I especially didn't like the thought of being the third wheel on my own birthday trip. I already had negative feelings toward this imaginary girlfriend. "Either way, I would never do something that would make the woman he was dating uncomfortable."

Camile pulled me into a hug. "Thanks for understanding, Madeline. I can see why Griffin likes you so much."

I patted Camile's back, but I couldn't quite make myself feel as happy as she was.

SIXTEEN
MADELINE

TUESDAY EVENING, I got home from work to find Harris sitting in his car in my driveway.

I hadn't heard anything from him since I'd left his house almost a week ago. Not a phone call or a text. Which was perfectly fine by me. It only made me more confused about what he was doing at my home.

I opened my garage door and pulled inside but didn't close it behind me, like I normally would.

I got out of my car the same time Harris exited his.

He had a smile on his face and flowers in his hand.

Standing there, stunned, I could only watch as he approached me.

"Harris, I didn't expect to see you."

"I thought we'd left things on bad terms last week."

When he reached me, he handed me the flowers and went to kiss me. Quickly, I turned my head, so he got my cheek instead of my lips.

Harris pursed his lips but didn't say anything about my brush-off.

"You might as well come in," I told him.

While I didn't really want him in my house because I wanted him to leave right away, it was cold out, and I didn't feel like shivering. Also, this would be a good time for me to give him back his things that he had left at my place. I had managed to pack it up over the weekend.

He followed me inside, and I went to my cupboards to find a vase for the flowers. I didn't appreciate his gesture, but it wasn't the flowers' fault.

"Smells good in here."

"Thanks," I said. "I put a roast in the Crock-Pot this morning." I loved coming home and not having to worry about cooking dinner.

"I love roast."

I looked over my shoulder at him in confusion from the sink, where I was filling the vase with water. "Since when?"

He shrugged. "Since forever."

I shook my head and went back to the flowers.

I didn't ever remember Harris liking roast before. I thought he had eaten it at my house once, and if I remembered correctly, he hadn't been too impressed.

"A home-cooked meal is always nice after being on the road."

Ah. Now, I understood. He was hinting at me to invite him for dinner.

That wasn't going to happen.

I finished putting the flowers in the vase and turned around. "I'm sorry. It's a small roast, and Griff is already coming over for dinner," I lied.

His lips pursed again. "I was hoping we could talk."

I sighed. "Harris, we don't really have anything to talk

about." I pushed away from the counter. "Give me a minute. I'll be right back."

I went to the guest bedroom, grabbed his box of junk I had collected, and brought it back to him. Setting it on the counter, I said, "Here is your stuff. If I forgot anything, let me know."

Hopefully, this would send a message loud and clear that I didn't want to talk to him about anything.

Harris went to the box, picked up a few things, and put them back. "I don't understand why things have to end. You and I had a good thing going."

I turned my head away and rolled my eyes. Taking a deep breath, I looked back at him. I put my hands together for emphasis. "Harris, you made no effort to celebrate my birthday, but even worse, you didn't even tell me you were going to be out of town until I asked. The worst part is, you weren't—and probably still aren't—even sorry."

"But I am sorry. The flowers are me apologizing."

I threw up my hands. "My birthday is only part of it." I used my fingers to start ticking off a list. "You don't like my friends, we haven't had sex in months, and we're just plain not right for each other."

"I like your friends," he protested. "And I would love to take you to bed right now."

I put my hand up. "No, thank you." I shuddered. "And you don't like my friends."

"Okay. Then, how about I make more of an effort to like them?"

I tilted my head to the side. "I don't understand. Why do you want to be with me so badly?"

"I like you, Madeline."

Yeah, well, I don't like you.

"Harris, we were together over a year, and you and I never said the words *I love you.*" I raised my eyebrows. "Don't you think that's a sign that things weren't great between us?"

"I think you and I only need more time."

I shook my head. "I think we had plenty of time." I didn't want to have this conversation anymore. "Did I forget anything?" I pointed to the box.

"No." Harris wasn't going to let me change the subject. "Will you at least have dinner with me this weekend?"

"No, thank you."

"If that's the way you want it," he said and marched toward my living room and what I assumed was out the front door. He could have just gone back the way he had come in through the garage, but I had to give it to Harris for being dramatic.

"You forgot your stuff," I said, realizing he'd left it on the counter. I chased after him. I really didn't want him to have an excuse to see me again.

But he wasn't going toward the front door; he was headed for the recliner in my living room.

I had to do something to end this.

"I had sex with someone else," I blurted out.

Harris paused and slowly pivoted. He cleared his throat. "When was this?"

"This weekend."

"Then, I forgive you," he said with a slight head nod.

"Uhhh...I don't need you to forgive me. We broke *up.*" I practically yelled the last word.

"Which is precisely why I forgive you. I think we can move past this hump in our relationship now that you got that out of your system." He turned back around and sat down. "Now, since you don't want to go to dinner, we can talk right here, right now."

I groaned and stomped back to the kitchen, where I'd left my purse. I pulled out my phone and began typing furiously.

SEVENTEEN

GRIFFIN

I HAD JUST POURED a drink for a customer when my phone buzzed twice in my pocket.

"Excuse me," I said and went to my office. I tried not to be on my phone at the bar unless I had to.

It was Madeline.

> Mads: 911! Harris was waiting in my driveway when I got home from work and now, he won't leave! He's determined to get back together. I even told him that I slept with someone else this weekend, and he still won't leave! Please help.

> Mads: P.S. I lied and told him you were eating dinner at my house. We're having roast beef.

I walked back out to the bar. "Mitch, I have a slight emergency. Can you handle things?"

Mitch looked around at the less than impressive Tuesday crowd. "I think I can manage," he said sarcastically.

"Good. Call Casey if you need help," I said as I pushed open the door.

"I was joking."

"I know."

I rushed to my car and pushed the speed limit all the way to Madeline's. I wasn't really worried that Harris would do anything to hurt her, but sometimes, previously decent guys lashed out.

When I got to her house, I pulled into the driveway behind Madeline. I'd wanted to park behind Harris simply to make his life more difficult, but that would defeat the purpose of getting him to leave.

I also had to resist the urge to key his car door as I walked toward the house.

I walked in through the garage without knocking and immediately noticed the flowers on the counter. They looked like some bouquet he had quickly grabbed off the shelf without any thought.

I could hear Harris talking in the living room. There wasn't any yelling, so I took that as a good sign.

I took my coat off and pulled up the sleeves of my long-sleeved shirt.

When I came around the corner, I saw Harris sitting with his legs crossed and speaking as if he were trying to sell something.

Madeline was sitting on the couch with her head leaning against the back and an arm over her eyes.

"What's going on here?" I asked.

Harris jumped, and Madeline sat up.

"Oh, thank God," she muttered.

I smiled at her reassuringly.

Harris turned in his seat. "If you don't mind, Madeline and I are having a discussion."

I walked around his chair until I faced him. "Yeah, well, it looks like Madeline doesn't want to have this conversation with you. I believe she told you that things were over between you two."

Harris stood and moved closer to me.

Madeline got up from the couch, but I held up my hand at my side to let her know I had this.

I gave Harris a deadpan look and crossed my arms. He wasn't the least bit intimidating. He was fit, but I was taller and had more muscle. I didn't want to brag, but if the we got in a fight, I could easily win.

"The two of us are none of your business, Griffin."

"It is when she texts me that you won't leave."

Harris turned his eyes to Madeline with an accusing look.

Out of the corner of my eye, I saw her turn her head away in guilt.

"Besides, Madeline and I have dinner plans tonight. You're kind of ruining them."

Harris clenched his jaw. "Madeline accused me of not liking her friends. But that's not exactly true. It's just you I don't like."

My brow went up. "Am I supposed to be offended by this? I don't like you either."

Eyes narrowing, he said, "You think you're so wonderful because you're the best friend. But that's all you'll ever be. Griffin Davis: permanent friend."

I looked at Madeline and pointed to Harris with my thumb. "Hey, Mads, Harris knows my last name." I tapped my forehead. "I think he's more bothered by us being friends than he lets on."

She looked at me with a half-smile, half-grimace expression.

I turned back to Harris and hoped that Madeline wouldn't be upset with me for what I was about to do.

The guy was like a dog with a bone, and he wasn't going to give up on Madeline if he thought that he had any sort of chance. I needed to make sure he knew he didn't have one.

I stepped forward. "What if I told you that Madeline and I are no longer just friends?"

Harris's eyes darted between Madeline and back to me several times. "Bullshit."

"I believe she told you that she slept with someone this weekend?"

"Yes, she did. But it wasn't you."

"Are you sure about that?"

He hesitantly raised his chin. "I am."

"Then, how do I know about the little mole on the inside of her thigh, right next to her pussy?"

Harris's eyes widened, and he lost some color to his face.

But I kept going. "Not even a best friend would know about that."

He swallowed.

"But maybe you don't know about the mole because you never bothered to pay that close of attention to her." I lifted a shoulder. "I mean, if you had, then she wouldn't have been asking me to make her come."

"You're lying," Harris hissed.

I chuckled. "No lie, man." I licked my bottom lip. "And holy shit, was it worth it. She's beautiful when she comes, am I right?" I grimaced. "Oh, sorry, I forgot, you couldn't make her do that." I patted him on the shoulder. "It's okay. You'll just have to take my word for it."

Harris surprised the hell out of me when he tried to take a swing at me.

But I was faster.

I caught his fist and pulled his arm behind his back as I got so close that our bodies touched. "Madeline doesn't want to be with you. The sooner you accept that, the sooner we can all move on because she's mine now. Got it? I don't let anyone touch what's mine."

I spun Harris around and led him to the front door.

"Don't show up here again," I said as I opened the door and pushed him out onto the front steps.

"Wait," Madeline said. "His stuff."

She ran to her kitchen and came back with a box.

I plucked it out of her hands and shoved it into Harris's chest. "Good-bye, Harris," I said and slammed the door in his face.

I took a deep breath and began preparing my apology to my best friend.

EIGHTEEN
MADELINE

I STOOD, stunned, as Griffin slowly turned around. I was actually surprised I had been able to collect my thoughts enough to remember to give Harris his box of stuff.

My best friend had a sheepish look as he faced me. "I'm sorry, Mads, for going all caveman. I didn't know how else to get rid of your stupid ex. I want you to know that I don't think any man can actually claim a woman as his. You belong to you, and even if we were dating, I would never think that I owned you or—"

I marched over to him and pulled him in for a kiss.

All tension left his body, and he grabbed my ass, pulling me close as he kissed me back.

"I probably shouldn't think this," I managed to say between me attacking his mouth, "but that was fucking hot as hell."

I felt him smile against my lips before he swept his tongue into my mouth.

I moaned and sucked on it. "Bedroom. Now," I managed to gasp out.

Griffin picked me up, and my legs went around his hips as he carried me to my room.

The two of us landed on the end of my bed, our bodies still intertwined. I squeezed my hands between our bodies, aiming for Griffin's fly. I didn't need any buildup; I'd had all the foreplay I required with all of Griffin's "she's mine" talk.

After some maneuvering, I managed to unbutton his pants and lower the zipper. I wrapped my fingers around his cock and squeezed.

He pulled his mouth away from mine with a gasp.

"Feel good?"

"Stupid question." He groaned as I pumped him. "You know it feels good."

I looked him in the eye. "I want you inside me, like yesterday."

He chuckled but lost his smile as his eyes rolled up in his head. "We need...fuck, Madeline, that feels good." Deep breath. "We need a condom."

I pointed up toward my head. "Nightstand drawer."

Griffin pulled off his shirt and kicked off his pants before crawling up my body. His dick bobbed right over my chest, so I lifted my head and licked the tip.

Such a shame I had forgotten to see what he tasted like on Friday.

It was a good thing I could remedy that right now.

I barely sucked the head in my mouth before it was taken away from me.

"Hey, I was playing with that," I said to his face when we were eye-level once again.

"Later. Right now, you need to take off your clothes, especially your pants."

I grinned. "Not until I get to play."

Griffin just lifted his brow and shook his head.

The next thing I knew, I was completely naked, and he was lying beside me, putting the condom on.

"How did you do that so fast?"

"Naked women are my specialty." He rolled back over me, and with one smooth thrust, he was inside me.

It was my turn for my eyes to roll back into my head.

"So wet. I love it," he said as he wrapped me in his arms.

I clutched wildly at his back as he began to move inside of me.

"Oh my God, right there," I panted.

How he'd hit the right spot so fast, I didn't know. Maybe naked women really were his specialty.

I widened my legs and lifted them toward Griffin's hips. I wanted him as deep as possible.

He must have sensed it because he took an arm and pushed my leg up over his elbow.

He continued to pound into me, his cock stretching me and rubbing my G-spot with every shift of his hips.

I felt my climax getting closer, but I didn't want this feeling to end. I wanted Griffin to keep fucking me forever.

Fortunately, best friends could read the other's body language, and they knew just what to do to make the other feel good when they were having sex. Unfortunately, best friends could read one's body language and knew when the other was about to come.

Griffin nipped my neck. "Come on, Mads. I know you're close. Quit holding out on me."

I let myself go, and my orgasm washed over me like

liquid heat. I was vaguely aware of Griffin still moving inside me, causing my climax to go on and on.

Just when I thought I couldn't take it anymore, he slammed into me one more time as his body stiffened and exploded.

The two of us lay there in silence. I could feel my inner muscles contracting every few seconds—the aftereffects of having a strong orgasm—and Griffin flinching every time it happened.

He slowly let my leg slide off his arm, and he rolled to my side. Putting a hand on my thigh, he asked, "You good?"

"God, yes."

He chuckled. "Good, because I'm fucking fantastic. Holy shit, no wonder Harris wants you back."

I groaned. "Don't talk about him. You'll ruin my post-orgasmic bliss."

He squeezed my leg. "Got it."

"Thank you. And thank you for coming when I texted. I was worried you hadn't gotten the messages."

"I will always come when you need me. And sorry about that. I left the bar so fast, I forgot to message back."

I smiled. "That's okay. The important thing is, you showed up. I don't know what I would have done to get rid of him if you hadn't." I hated to think that I could still be sitting in my living room as Harris tried to pitch me on why we should be together.

"There was something else you texted me about."

I frowned. "What's that?"

He got up on one elbow and smiled down at me. "Correct me if I'm wrong, but I think you said I was invited to dinner."

NINETEEN
MADELINE

THE NEXT MORNING, I was leaning against my counter as I sipped my coffee and scrolled through various social media apps on my phone.

I was laughing at a meme when Griffin walked into the kitchen in only a pair of jeans.

I tried not to look too hard at all his gorgeous muscles. It was funny how I had seen Griffin shirtless plenty of times, but now that we'd had sex, all I could think was that I wanted to touch him, I wanted to feel him, I wanted to—

"Got any coffee for me?"

I blinked a couple times as I tried to erase all sexual thoughts of my best friend from my brain.

Griffin raised his brow. "Tired?"

"A little." I nodded toward the coffeepot. "I made extra for you." I looked at the clock on the microwave. "Although I'm surprised you're up before I have to leave for work."

He found a mug and poured himself a cup. "It helps that I didn't close the bar last night and got a good night's sleep." He smiled at me over the coffee he had brought to his lips and winked. "For the most part anyway."

My pussy clenched.

You don't have time for morning sex, you don't have time for morning sex, you don't have time for morning sex.

I still had to take a shower and get ready.

"Screw it," I said, setting my coffee down. I took Griffin's mug from his hand and set it next to mine. "Fuck me in the shower?" I asked.

He grinned. "You don't have to ask me twice," he said and picked me up in his arms.

I squealed as he sprinted toward the bathroom.

Half an hour later, I reluctantly put on my work clothes and makeup. My limbs felt like jelly, and my mind was mush. I was going to be useless at work.

After I was finished getting ready, I went back to the kitchen with my dirty mug. Griffin had kindly brought me some coffee while I was busy making myself presentable for work.

He was my best friend for a reason after all.

"When do you have to leave?" he asked me.

I checked the time again. "Five minutes. Which is good. I thought for sure that I was going to be late when I asked you to shower with me."

He put a hand on his chest. "Aww, and you asked me anyway."

I rolled my eyes. "Don't get a big head. I like morning sex, and you were available."

This time, he brought his fist to his chest like I had stabbed him. "The pain. It hurts."

I pushed him out of the way and put my cup in the dishwasher. "You'll be fine."

He dumped out his mug in the sink and put it next to mine in the machine. "What are you doing this weekend? Are you stopping by the bar tonight?"

"I'm not sure, and maybe. I was thinking of using my birthday gift cards this weekend, so we'll have to see if I feel like shopping."

Griffin put on his shoes and shrugged his large arms into his coat. "Count me in."

"You want to go to the bookstore with me?" I asked, surprised.

Griffin wasn't much of a reader.

"Ha. No. I want to go to the lingerie store with you."

"Yeah, that's not going to happen." Fluorescent lights were brutal on the body. I had pretty good self-esteem when it came to my looks, but I thought fluorescent lights could make the perfect woman have doubts about herself.

"After I came to your rescue?"

I picked up my purse. "Are you saying I owe you?"

I had to admit that I was grateful for Griffin's help with Harris yesterday. And I had been pretty excited when he actually stayed for dinner and didn't leave once to go and check on his bar. When I'd joked the other night about the bar being his wife, I had been half-serious. It took a lot to pull him away from that place.

He looked at me with puppy-dog eyes. "No. Only saying it would be nice if you took your best friend with you."

I sighed. "I'll think about it. But you do realize, you

can't go into the dressing room with me, so you're not going to know what any of the stuff I try on looks like, right?"

He grinned and opened the door to the garage. "You just let me worry about that."

I went to walk past him and stopped to shove a finger in his face. "I'm not taking pictures either and sending them to you." I didn't want to risk getting hacked and having embarrassing pictures of me all over the internet.

He nipped my finger. "I told you to let me worry about that."

"Okay." I continued into the garage and hit the door opener. I threw my purse in my car and turned around to say good-bye.

I wasn't expecting Griffin to be right behind me, and I squeaked as he pushed me against the driver's door. I clutched the sides of his shirt under his coat, unsure of what he was going to do.

"Have a good day at work," he said.

"Thanks. You have a good day at work too."

"I will now." He leaned in and took my mouth. He kissed me deep and slow, taking his time. By the time he pulled away, I was breathless. "Thanks for the morning fuck." He smiled. "And all the times last night."

"You're welcome?" I laughed. "I mean, it's not like I got anything out of it, so you definitely owe me one."

He chuckled. "Yeah, I do. I promised you could play with my dick, and I still haven't let you. Maybe this weekend after shopping. You can buy the sluttiest outfit, and I'll let you wear it while you go down on me."

"You'll 'let' me? You are so full of shit."

He grinned. "I try." He squeezed my hips, and his face got more serious. "I'll see you later?"

"Yeah," I said with a nod.

He kissed me again and headed to his car.

He waved as he got behind the wheel, and I was reminded that I needed to get in my own vehicle and get my butt to work.

As I started my car and headed down my driveway, I thought about the change in my relationship with Griffin. I didn't know if we were going to continue to sleep with each other or what would happen when we stopped, and I decided I would worry about that later.

TWENTY
GRIFFIN

WEDNESDAY EVENING, I was waiting for Madeline to show when two of my old friends came in.

I had met Caleb and Blake in little league. They were both older than me, but we had stayed friends throughout the years, even when Caleb had gone to Europe for a year and Blake had moved to Las Vegas for a while.

"Hey," I greeted them. "Table or bar?"

"Bar's fine," Caleb said.

"Nothing big on your mind?" I asked. Whenever one of us needed more privacy, we would get a table to be farther away from accidental eavesdroppers.

"Nah," Caleb said as he sat down. "Life's good."

"And you, Blake?"

"Nothing new for me," he said, taking a seat beside Caleb.

"The usual?" I asked them.

They both said yes, and I slid their beers over to them. "I wasn't expecting to see either of you tonight."

"Last-minute visit. I can only stay for a beer before I have to get home."

"Sloan won't let you stay out late, huh?" Blake asked him.

Caleb frowned. "No. My brother's coming over."

"Oh."

I laughed. "Poor Blake. He just wants to give someone shit."

He narrowed his eyes at me. "Keep it up, and you'll be my next target."

I just grinned back.

The door opened again, and Madeline walked through. "Hey, guys," she said before coming around and sitting by Blake. I would have preferred she sat down next to Caleb, the married guy.

I pulled out a beer and set it in front of her. "Happy one-week anniversary," I told her.

Caleb leaned forward around Blake. "One week? For what?"

Madeline looked at me, confused.

"For breaking up with that asshole, Harris."

She laughed and picked up her beer. "I'll drink to that. Good riddance."

"This sounds like a good story," Blake said.

"Meh. He blew off my birthday and didn't even remember what day it was."

Blake and Caleb winced.

"Ouch," Blake said.

"Oh, and happy late birthday," Caleb added.

"Yeah, happy late birthday," Blake said. "I hope you had fun."

"Thanks. I did." Madeline swung her stool in my direction and smiled at me.

While I'd known her for years, this particular smile was new to me. But it didn't take a genius to guess what she was thinking about.

Sex.

Madeline was thinking about sex.

And now, so was I.

I maintained eye contact while I reached down and adjusted myself since I was hard. The bar hid everything lower torso and down, but she was a smart girl. She could figure out exactly what I was doing.

"Griff?" she said in an almost-too-innocent voice.

"Yeah?"

"I need to talk to you in your office. Do you have a minute?"

"Uh-oh, Griffin's in trouble," Blake joked.

I shook my head at the ridiculous statement.

"No, he's not in trouble. It's just private. Between best friends," Madeline said and slid off her stool.

"I'm so hurt, Griffy. I thought I was your best friend."

I took the rag I had on my shoulder and tossed it on the bar. "Blake, you know I have better taste than that," I joked and headed back toward my office.

Madeline had already gone up ahead of me.

I pushed open the door, and the room was dark, except for the night-light I kept in the corner.

I reached for the light switch, but I was yanked inside by my shirt and slammed against the door before I could reach it.

I hoped nobody came to see if we were okay.

Madeline's mouth was immediately on mine as she went after my pants. The woman was fast—I had to give her that —because she had my dick out and in her hands before I could put more thoughts together.

She squeezed me once, and then her lips were gone, and so was she.

I looked down to see her on her knees and her mouth swallowing my cock.

"Oh fuck. Fuck, fuck, fuck, fuck, fuck."

Watching and feeling my best friend suck on me was the hottest thing I'd ever seen in my life.

Which didn't bode well for my lasting ability. Not to mention, she was really good at giving head.

I shouldn't be surprised since she excelled at sex, but I didn't like that she had learned all her amazing techniques on someone other than me.

But my jealousy wasn't enough for me to lose my hard-on or anything. It only made me want to come in her mouth even more. I wanted to be the last thing she tasted on her tongue.

And I was about to let her do that as I leaned back and enjoyed the ride—until I noticed that she was shifting a lot.

Madeline was getting all hot and horny from giving me a blow job.

I was two seconds away from exploding, and if I wanted Madeline to get off too, then I had to cut off this particular event off now.

And with that, I cupped the back of her head and pulled her mouth away from me.

"Wha—" she said, stunned, as I yanked her to her feet.

I twirled her around, so her back was against the door as I pushed her jeans off her legs and threw the pants to the side.

Not only did I want to know how she tasted now—I mean, in reality, I'd wanted to know how she tasted since I discovered eating women out in high school—but I also needed a little bit of time to make sure I didn't pull a two-pump-and-dump the second I got inside her.

I dropped down to my knees and pulled her leg over my shoulder. I swiped a finger over her cleft. She was already wet, just like I had suspected, and I leaned forward and licked her from back to front, stopping at her clit to run my tongue around it.

Madeline whimpered, and I knew I should concentrate my attention on making her come, but I wanted to do my own thing.

Cupping her ass, I shoved my face between her legs. I licked and sucked on every inch of skin I came into contact with. I loved her musky scent and the way her flavor tasted in my mouth.

I could admit, I was being a little selfish, but in all truth, I wasn't sure how long this sexual relationship was going to last. And if this was the only time I went down on my best friend, I wasn't going to waste it. So, because I was so caught up in my own needs, I didn't notice Madeline trying to push me away at first.

And when I did, I felt incredibly guilty.

"Holy shit. Mads, I'm so—"

She pushed me onto my back on the floor and straddled my hips, and in one smooth move, I was inside her.

I groaned from deep in my throat and grasped her hips.

I'd thought the blow job felt good, but her pussy felt fucking amazing. I didn't understand why at the moment, nor did I have time to figure it out because she began to ride me.

She had only pushed me away because she wanted to fuck me. And wasn't that the turn-on of the century?

I pulled on her hips as I tried to help, so she didn't get tired or worn out.

But I didn't need to worry about that.

It wasn't long before her breathing changed and she started tightening around me. I also noticed that the closer she got, the wetter she got. I had never observed that before, which was odd. It was hot as hell, and I would think that I wouldn't have missed something like this.

Madeline was almost there, her nails digging into my shoulders and her head thrown back when it hit me.

I wasn't wearing a condom.

"Shit. Mads, I'm not—"

Too late. She cried out as her whole body jerked over me. This wasn't just a leg-shaking orgasm. This was a whole-body-shaking orgasm.

And I tried to do everything I could to stop my own climax. I bit down hard on my lip, and I tried to think about anything other than how incredible it felt to be inside Madeline bare.

Raw.

"Fuck." I felt bad, cutting Madeline's orgasm short, but I had to get her off me. "Madeline, I'm not wearing a—"

Boom.

It was too late.

I exploded so hard, to the point I saw stars and then my vision went black. My hands let go of Madeline's hips and fell to my sides, and I rode wave after wave of bliss.

TWENTY-ONE
GRIFFIN

I DIDN'T KNOW how long it took for my brain to come back online after that hard reset, but when I did, I noticed that Madeline was lying on me and my ass was freezing from the cold floor.

Oh, and I was still inside her, and we were both covered in my cum.

I gently rolled her off me and to her side before I slid out from her body. "Madeline, I wasn't wearing a condom."

Her eyes snapped open, and she sat up so fast that her head almost hit my nose. "Oh shit."

"I know."

She spread her legs, and even though it was mostly dark, she must have been able to tell something I couldn't.

"Damn, Griff, are you trying to get me pregnant? I have never had so much semen in me."

"Sorry."

"No, you're not. That comment went straight to your head."

"Well, I am a guy, and you basically just complimented

124

my virility," I told her as I opened the closet in the corner. I pulled out a clean towel we used for the bar and handed it to her.

I tucked my half-hard dick back into my pants and got down on my haunches. "You're not really going to get…"

Madeline looked up at me. "Pregnant? No, I'm on birth control."

I fell back on my butt in relief. "Oh, thank God."

"But when's the last time you got tested?" Madeline asked. "I know I haven't been since Harris and I broke up. I'm not worried, but still. It's something we should both do now that you've hosed me down with your freaking seed."

I laughed. "I didn't come that much."

"You're not the one drowning in it."

"I'm sorry. What can I do to help?"

"Get my purse. I think I have a pad in there."

"Like, for your period?"

She blinked at me. "Or for when you're going to have semen coming out of your pussy for the next couple of hours."

I jumped to my feet. "Purse. I'm on it."

I turned on the light and hurried out to where Madeline had left her purse by Blake and Caleb.

"Hey, where are you going?" Blake said.

I snatched the purse up and said, "I'll be right back."

When I got back to the office, Madeline was standing up and wiping her thighs.

She looked up when she saw me. "Could you get me a wet towel? I'd go to the restroom, but I'm not wearing any pants."

I grabbed a towel from the closet. "Be right back."

I could have gone to the bar again but chose the restroom instead. I didn't want Caleb and Blake to question why I was going back and forth.

I brought the towel back. "Is there anything else I can do to help?"

Madeline took it from me. "No, I think I'm good now."

"Are you okay?" I asked. I really wanted to know if she was mad at me, but I couldn't quite bring myself to ask that.

"I'll be fine. But the two of us need to get tested right away, okay?"

"I'll make an appointment with my doctor tomorrow morning when the clinic opens," I promised.

"Same." She tilted her head toward the door. "Now, get out of here, so I can finish cleaning up in private."

I nodded and left her alone.

I needed a drink after everything that had happened. When I got back behind the bar, I lined up three shot glasses and filled them all with my favorite whiskey.

I set two of them in front of my friends and downed my own.

Blake tipped his head back and swallowed his down, but Caleb stared at me.

"Are you okay?" he asked.

Now that the adrenaline had worn off, everything was becoming clearer, and I was a little freaked out.

"Depends on your definition of okay." I chuckled. Just an impromptu sex session in my place of business that was my livelihood and a pregnancy and STI scare. I supposed I was okay. The customers weren't the wiser, and Madeline was on birth control. I sighed. "Yeah, I'm fine."

"Everything okay with Madeline?"

"Yeah. Why?"

"Because you keep looking back toward your office," Caleb said.

"Dude, you're not boning your bestie, are you?" Blake asked.

I narrowed my eyes at him. "Jesus, Blake, a little class?"

"Thank God," he said.

"Why do you say that?" Caleb asked.

"Because friends with benefits almost never works. One of them usually gets too emotionally involved, and then the friendship is over because the other doesn't want to get serious. I know two couples it worked for. In one, they both sincerely didn't want to get serious. They're both married to other people, and they're still friends. The other, they both wanted to take their relationship to the next level, and they're married. But I find both of those are the exception, not the rule."

"How many people do you know?" Caleb asked.

"A lot. I lived in Vegas, remember? The capital of drunk friends getting married and then calling things off." Blake looked at me. "All I'm saying is, the two of you have been friends forever. Do you really want to ruin that for some nookie?"

"That's surprisingly wise, coming from you," I joked because I didn't want to think about what he'd said.

Madeline was my best friend, and I didn't want to lose her just because we were both a little horny.

What have I done?

Madeline came back, looking the same as when she'd left the three of us earlier.

"Everything good?" I asked her.

"Yep," she said, getting back on her stool. "Can I get some water?"

"Coming right up."

"So, what did you and Griffin talk about?" Blake asked her, wiggling his eyebrows.

"Wouldn't you like to know?" she said with a smile.

"Duh. That's why I'm asking."

She looked at him over the water I'd poured for her. "And that's the way we're going to keep it."

"You're no fun."

"Hey, Madeline, did you get anything good for your birthday?" Caleb said. He was probably trying to change the subject, so Blake would stop bothering her.

"Yes. Lots of money and gift cards. Everyone knows me so well."

"We know she likes to pick out her own things," I added.

"Exactly. This is why I have to tell Griffin what to buy me every year."

"And what did he get you this year?" Caleb asked.

"I couldn't believe it. He got me—"

"I got her a gift card too."

She frowned in confusion and looked at me.

I didn't have the balls to meet her eyes. "In my defense, she didn't tell me what to get her even though I had asked." I shrugged. "So, she got a gift card."

"Boo," Blake said. "So boring."

"I know," I admitted.

I could feel Madeline's eyes on me, but I avoided them as much as possible. I couldn't tell her that Blake had worried me. And I didn't know how to tell her that I thought we shouldn't sleep together anymore before things went too far. Not after we just had sex. It felt like I was using her even if she had initiated it. I hadn't exactly put a stop to it.

I licked my lips and caught a taste of Madeline on the upper one. I wished I had taken more time going down on her since it wasn't going to happen again.

TWENTY-TWO

MADELINE

FRIDAY EVENING, I was sitting on a plush white sofa, drinking champagne, while I watched Christina do a fitting of her wedding dress.

Her sister and maid of honor, Hope, was running the show, so I was sitting and listening to her go over wedding things.

It sounded exhausting, and if I ever got married, I was going to have a small wedding or get married at the courthouse.

"After Troy's brother and me, it'll be you and Griffin, then—"

"I'm sorry," I interrupted Hope. "What are you talking about?"

"The procession line."

"I told Hope that Troy and I wanted you and Griffin after the maid of honor and best man. If it wasn't for the two of you, we wouldn't have met."

I grinned. "I love it." And I loved that I wouldn't have to walk down the aisle with a stranger.

Hope listed off everyone else as Christina did a couple of twirls in her dress. "Did I get everything correct?" she asked.

"Yes." Christina turned to look at her sister. "But what if Mom asks to look at the list?"

Hope pulled out another sheet from her binder and grinned. "I got that covered."

"Can I see?" I asked.

She handed over both lists, and I scanned the names. The first list said I was second after Hope. This one said I was following behind Chantel. "Who's Chantel?"

"Our cousin," Hope said. "And Mom is forcing Christina to put her in the wedding."

"I'm only doing it to make my mom happy. And Chantel is not going to be happy when she finds out that she's last." Her smile was a little evil, and I laughed.

"She's that bad, huh?" I asked.

"Horrible. Stuck-up and has always thought she is too good. I was shocked that she even said yes. The only reason I'd asked her was because I thought she'd say no *and* it would make my mom happy."

My phone's message tone I had set just for Griffin went off in my purse, so I pulled it out.

Griffin: I know we have plans tomorrow, but I can't make it now.

I frowned.

Me: Can I ask why?

"What's wrong?" Christina asked.

131

I looked up. "Griffin. He's been acting strange since Wednesday." Since the day we'd slept together.

I had gone to the doctor right away and gotten tested. When I'd told him, he'd barely said two words to me.

I was worried that I had scared him with my pregnancy joke or that he thought I was mad at him.

I had been a little irritated that we had forgotten protection, but the frustration was at both of us and the situation. I had tried to show him that I wasn't mad.

I couldn't figure out what had happened between him leaving his office and me coming back to the bar.

I had considered that he'd told Caleb and Blake what happened, and they had given him crap about it. But there was no way Blake would know something like that and not make even one joke about it to me. Besides, neither of them had given me curious looks or anything like they had been let in on a secret.

No, I was ninety-nine percent sure Griffin hadn't said anything.

Which left me back where I'd started. Griffin had been acting odd, and now, he was canceling on me. And the plans were his idea.

Griffin: Troy needs help with something.

"And now, Griffin is canceling our plans tomorrow, so he can hang out with Troy," I told Christina. I met her eyes. "He's not lying to me, is he?"

Hope looked confused. "You and Griffin are dating?"

I shook my head. "No. We're really good friends."

"Oh. Okay."

"Hope, will you hand me my phone?" Christina asked.

Hope moved some stuff around on the sofa, grabbed Christina's phone, and handed it to her.

She started typing.

"What are you doing?" I asked.

"Asking Troy if he has any plans on Saturday. We'll see if he brings up Griffin's name."

"Good idea," I said and started tapping my foot.

Thankfully, Troy answered right away.

Christina looked at her phone. "He says that he and Griffin do have plans."

I breathed a sigh of relief. He hadn't lied to me.

Christina's phone beeped again.

"Oh."

"Oh? Oh what?" I pressed her.

"He said that Griffin asked him if he wanted to do anything. Troy was going to tell him no because he had a rough week at work, but Griffin insisted. Then, he said, *The things I do for friends.*"

Christina and Hope both watched me. I supposed to see what kind of reaction I would have.

I opened up my message thread with Griffin. I was mad and upset. He had never blown me off before. But I didn't want him to know I had checked up on him. Not because he'd be mad, but because I didn't want him to know I cared so much since he obviously didn't care that much back.

I had to wonder if this was the beginning of the end of our friendship.

Me: Have fun.

"What did you say?" Christina asked.

I shrugged. "I told him to have fun."

She looked at me like I was crazy. "If you canceled plans on me like that and begged April or someone else to hang out with you, I'd be pissed."

"Oh, I'm pissed. I just don't want him to know."

"Why?" Hope asked.

"Because revenge is never as much fun if the other person knows it's coming."

Christina laughed. "Ooh. What were you going to go and do tomorrow?"

"Go shopping."

"Shopping? No wonder Griffin canceled."

"It was his idea," I defended myself. "I was going to go and use my gift card for lingerie."

"Are you sure you two are just friends?" Hope asked.

"A single guy helping his best girl friend in a lingerie shop is an excellent way to attract women," I fibbed. It wasn't the real reason he had wanted to come with me, but it was true. When women saw a guy doting on his partner, they thought it was sweet. When they found out he was the single friend, they thought it was hot.

"Ah," Hope said.

"Maybe I'll go shopping with you tomorrow instead," Christina said. "And maybe I'll send Troy some pics while we're there with some beautiful shoppers in the background, and maybe he'll show Griffin everything he's missing."

I laughed. "I like the way you think."

Meanwhile, I would share a couple of pictures of my own. I was going to make sure Griffin *knew* what he was missing.

TWENTY-THREE

GRIFFIN

"SHOULD we go get something to eat?" Troy asked me.

"Sure." It wasn't like we had anything else to do.

I had come over to Troy and Christina's place an hour or so ago, and so far, Troy and I had sat on his couch and played video games.

"Aren't you hungry?" Troy asked me.

I shrugged. "Not really."

The guilt I felt about lying to Madeline had made me lose my appetite. I should have just told her the truth. That I thought we were getting too close and that it wasn't a good idea. Instead, I had made up a story that Troy needed help with something.

He didn't need help with anything. So far, we'd done nothing productive.

"Well, I'm starving. It's almost one, so I say we get out of here."

"Okay. Let me hit the head first."

I was in the middle of washing my hands when I heard Troy speaking to someone else.

"Ooh, I think you should get that one."

I walked out of the bathroom to see him holding his phone in front of him.

"Model it for me," he said with a grin.

"Who are you talking to? I sure hope that's Christina," I joked.

He flashed me the screen for a second. "Christina and Madeline."

Upon hearing Madeline's name, I walked around the back of the couch, so I could see over Troy's shoulder.

Christina was holding up two baby-doll lingerie sets, which probably meant that Madeline was holding the phone.

"White or black?" Christina asked.

"Both," Troy answered.

"Sorry, no can do. They're not cheap, and I want to buy some other stuff. So, you have to pick one."

"Hmm…surprise me."

Christina didn't look impressed. She looked up and over her phone. "What do you think, Madeline?"

"Hold them up in front of you."

Christina did just that.

"I'd go with black," I said.

Christina grinned. "Thanks, Griff," she said while her fiancé gave me a dirty look over his shoulder.

"What? You weren't picking one, so I did." I patted him on the shoulder. "You'll thank me later."

Christina grabbed her phone after hanging the white teddy up. "Since you're so helpful, Griffin, maybe you can help Madeline decide which one to get too." She rolled her eyes. "Madeline is being way more difficult than me though."

"I am not."

Christina nodded at us through the phone.

"Just turn the camera around, so I can show them," Madeline said.

The camera flipped to show Madeline against a rack of bras with three different teddies that she had hung up in front for us to see. They were much more revealing than Christina's pick, and my heart sped up.

"They're all the same style, but I can't decide between black, white, or red. Black is classic, white has the whole *innocent but not really innocent* vibe, and red...well, red is sexy."

"Hold them up in front of you," Christina suggested.

"Try them on and send pics," I blurted out.

Madeline leaned into the camera. "I don't think so." She backed up, pulled each teddy off the rack, and held them up in front of her.

Meanwhile, I pulled out my phone and sent her a text.

> Me: I need to see pics.

I heard Madeline's phone beep through Christina's phone.

"Hold, please," she said.

Christina turned her camera back around and asked Troy something about Sunday. I wasn't paying attention because I was waiting for Madeline's response.

> Madeline: So you can jerk off to them later?

Madeline: I don't think so.

Me: No, so I can tell you what to buy. I can't tell you what to get when you only hold them up in front of you.

Me: Please.

Madeline: Sorry, dude. If you wanted to see it in person, you shouldn't have canceled on me.

Me: This isn't fair.

Madeline: Life's not fair. But maybe Troy has something sexy he can put on for you.

"I'm done," Madeline said in the background. "If Griff and Troy don't have any opinions, I think I'm going to go with white."

"I'd better go," Christina said to Troy.

"Not white. Red," I shouted, but the call was already cut.

I sent Madeline a text, telling her to get red, but she didn't even open my message.

"Let's go," I said to Troy.

Troy's face lit up. "We're going to go and get food?"

"No, we're going to the mall." I grabbed my keys off the coffee table, where I'd thrown them down when I got there.

"But I'm hungry," Troy whined.

"You can get something at the food court. We need to go now."

"I have half a mind to tell you to go by yourself."

"But then you won't be able to have Christina try on her little outfit for you."

He shrugged. "She'll try it on when she gets home."

I shook my head sadly. "You're not even married yet, and you'd rather eat than see your beautiful woman half-naked."

Troy gritted his teeth. "Fine. We'll go to the mall. While my dick thanks you, my stomach is really pissed at you."

"Grab a piece of fruit or something," I told him. "It'll tide you over until we get there."

TWENTY-FOUR
MADELINE

"YOU OKAY?" Christina asked me as she bumped her hip into mine.

I was going through a drawer of panties, looking for my size. "Yeah. Why?"

"Because you seem kind of bummed."

"No," I lied. "Just forgot how exhausting shopping for this stuff is. Men have it so easy. Boxers, briefs, boxer briefs. Women have bikini, high cut, thong, boy cut, full cut, briefs, et cetera. And sexy is nice, but most days, I want something comfortable that's not going to give me a wedgie at work."

"I hear ya."

"Don't tell April, okay? I don't want her to think I don't appreciate my birthday present."

Christina pretended to zip up her lips.

"Thank you."

She nodded down at my hands. "I thought you'd decided on the white? Yet you're still holding all three."

"I know. But I still need to try them on, and what if I'm

in there and I decide I don't like the white? This way, I'll already have the other colors."

"Smart. Maybe I shouldn't have put mine back."

"Go get it, and we can go try our stuff on. I'm done with this store anyway. I want to use my other gift card now."

"Good-bye, lingerie. Hello, books," she said.

I chuckled. "Exactly. But take your time. It's going to take me a few minutes to get myself in and out of these things," I said, holding up the teddies. "And I don't want to rip anything."

"Let's go find someone to get us rooms."

The dressing rooms were in their own little hall. Unfortunately, it was a Saturday, so we had to take what was open. Christina ended up at the front, and I had to take the room in the back corner.

My phone rang. It was Christina.

"I guess we won't be showing each other how the lingerie looks," she said with disappointment. "I'm not walking down to your dressing room, half-naked."

"I understand." It would have been nice to be right across the hall from each other to limit our exposure. "I don't want to walk up there either. We'll have to stick to our own judgments, I guess."

"Good luck," she told me.

"Good luck to you too."

I hit End and picked the white teddy first. I didn't even need Christina to tell me that it was the wrong choice. I looked washed out, and I was glad I'd decided to try on stuff before I purchased anything.

But I did decide not to waste a good opportunity.

I picked up my phone and turned the camera on. I took zoomed-in pictures of my body. I did my hip with some lace showing. Next, I did a shoulder with a strap. Then, I sent the pictures to Griffin.

> Me: Here are the pics you asked for.

I laughed as I hit Send. Sometimes, I thought I was really funny.

I set my cell aside and looked at my other two options. I wasn't sure how red would look on me, so I opted for the black teddy next.

It occurred to me that maybe I should have brought in more styles in case I didn't like any of them. I really hadn't been thinking as ahead as I thought I had.

"Madeline?"

I paused mid-change. I thought I'd heard my name.

"Madeline?" It was closer this time.

I quickly pulled the straps up on the black teddy and opened the door a crack.

It was Griffin.

"Madeline?" he said again, his back to me.

I didn't know if I wanted him to know where I was, but another woman stepped out of her dressing room and gave him a dirty look.

"Psst," I said. "I'm over here."

Griffin spun around and looked relieved to see me.

"What are you doing here?" I asked him when he reached my room.

"I came to help."

"Your help is no longer needed."

"Come on, Mads. Let me in."

I narrowed my eyes. "I don't think you deserve to be let in."

He frowned. "Why do you say that?"

"Because you blew me off today."

"I'm so—"

I held my hand up. "And you lied to me."

He closed his mouth and swallowed.

"I know you asked Troy to hang out. Next time, ask a friend who's not engaged to my friend."

He took a deep breath. "Okay, so you have to let me in, so I can explain." He put a hand over his eyes. "I promise not to look at you."

I rolled my eyes, opened the door, and pulled him inside by his other hand. His elbow hit the doorjamb as he stepped inside.

"Ow."

"Sorry," I said as I closed the door behind him.

"You don't sound sorry."

"Eh. You get what you deserve."

"Mads"—he dropped his hand and turned around—"I really am—" His eyes widened. "Holy shit, you look fucking hot."

I stepped around him and pulled my shirt in front of me. "You said you weren't going to look."

He put his hand back in front of his eyes. "You're right. But I will never get rid of the image of you in that." He separated his fingers and peeked through them. "And for that, I'm not sorry."

I crossed my arms over my chest.

His fingers slammed closed.

143

"Okay, you may speak now."

"On Wednesday, after I left my office, Blake and Caleb asked me if anything was going on between us."

This caught my attention. "They know?"

Griffin frowned. "And that's a bad thing?"

"I don't know. I'd be fine with Caleb knowing, but Blake would give us so much crap that I'd prefer to avoid."

"This is true. But I didn't tell them yes."

"Is this why you didn't want them to know what you got me for my birthday?"

At the time, I hadn't understood why he didn't want them to know. He should be proud of his awesome present, and it was odd that he'd lied about it.

"Yes. But let me finish, please."

"Continue."

"Blake started talking about how friends with benefits never work. He's seen a lot of friendships break up because of it, and it scared me." He dropped his hand. "You're my best friend, Mads. I don't want to lose you."

I tilted my head and studied him. "So, your idea was to push me away in order to not lose me?"

Griff rubbed the back of his neck and chuckled nervously. "When you put it like that…"

"You sound like a doofus?"

"Hey." He dropped his arm and stood up straight.

"Maybe those friendships broke up because one person thought they knew what was better for the other." I raised my brow. "Did you ever think of that?"

"Jeez, Mads, how did you get so smart?"

"Quit trying to butter me up."

He grinned.

"Seriously though, Griff. We tell each other everything. I know about the time you shit your pants in psych class after being hungover."

He shook his head. "You promised to never speak of that again."

"And I haven't until now." I poked him in the chest. "And you know about the time I took that guy home, and I didn't know I had my period, so when we turned on the lights, the guy freaked out because he thought I was dying while I just wanted to literally die from embarrassment."

Griffin laughed. "That is kind of a funny story."

"You weren't there." I waved my hand back and forth. "That's not the point. The point is, if we can talk about shit and periods, we can talk about our friendship. Okay?"

"Okay," he agreed with a nod.

"So, from here on out, we'll just go back to being friends."

He scowled. "I never said that."

"Oh?" I bit the inside of my lip so that I wouldn't smile. "You want to keep having sex?"

"Damn right I do." He grabbed my wrists and pulled my arms wide. "And right now, I want to see you model for me. The pictures you sent me were just plain mean."

I lifted a shoulder. "I didn't look good in white anyway."

"Let me see the red." He licked his lips. "And I'll let you know which one I'll be taking off you later."

"That sounds like a cheesy pickup line."

"It's only cheesy if it's never going to happen. *I'm* totally going to make that happen tonight."

TWENTY-FIVE
MADELINE

I HEARD the door to Griffin's apartment open and close and his footsteps move closer to his bedroom. I rolled onto my back, and he pushed the half-closed door open.

Rubbing my eyes, I asked, "Closing go okay?"

"Yep. No troubles tonight. Everyone left when we told them to."

I watched as Griffin stripped off his clothes. His room was dark, but I could see plenty, thanks to electronics and streetlights lighting up his room.

When he was naked, he literally jumped into bed with me and pulled the covers over himself.

He snuggled up against me and ran his hands over my body. "Ooh, naked best friend."

"I haven't moved since you left," I told him. Besides, I wasn't going to put my teddy—which was lying on the floor next to his bed—on again, and my other clothes were in his living room.

"You've been sleeping this whole time?" He yawned and moved to his back. "I'm jealous."

"Not the whole time. I did spend an unhealthy amount of time on social media." I rolled from my back to my side and slid my leg over his. "But I did go to sleep earlier than usual. I think something wore me out."

His eyes were closed, but he smiled. "Same here. I was dragging ass by the end of the night. Or the end of this morning? Whatever. You know what I mean."

"I'm sorry."

"No, you're not. You probably think I deserve it."

When I didn't respond, he opened one eye and lifted his head to look at me.

I held my finger and thumb up with a small space between them. "A little bit."

He laughed and dropped his head back onto the pillow. "I have bad news."

"Oh? What's that?"

"I'm about two seconds away from falling asleep, so if you want any sex, you'd better hop on this ride before it's off for the night."

I ran my hands down his body. "But you're not even—" I found his penis thick and hard. "Never mind."

"I'm always hard when you're around."

I wrapped my hand around him, definitely game for some sex now that I'd had a nap. But I wasn't going to do that to him. He was too tired, and even though he seemed willing, I thought it would be nicer of me to let him sleep.

"Mmm…that feels good."

I kissed his chest and reluctantly let his dick go. "When you said you're always hard when I'm around, when did that start? My birthday party night? Or right after?"

He shifted his hips as he seemed to settle in more. "Before that."

This had my full attention, and if I hadn't been wide awake, I was now. "How long before?" I asked in a low, soothing voice. I didn't want him to know this had caught my interest.

"Since forever."

"Forever?" I said a little too loud.

Griffin laughed. "Not forever. I didn't care about girls being girls when we first started being friends. But as soon as I hit puberty."

I had been wrong earlier in the day. Apparently, the two of us didn't tell each other everything.

"Wow," I said.

"Not wow. More like duh. You're hot."

I tried to run through decades of friendship in my head to see if anything stuck out to me. A time where Griffin might have been turned on and I might have suspected.

But nothing was coming to mind.

At first.

I gasped. "Remember that time about five years ago when we were at the water park and we went down the slide together?"

"Mmm."

I took that as a yes.

"You told me you were hard because of the adrenaline of going down the slides." He had gone down several in a row. "Were you lying?"

"Mmm."

I shook him. "Griffin?"

"What?"

"Were you lying?"

"Through my teeth. You wore that green bikini. I never knew green could be so hot."

I bit my lip. It had been more like a tankini. I wasn't trying to be sexy. I had just wanted to be comfortable at the water park.

"I can't believe you never told me."

"I didn't want to freak you out."

I could understand that. It was always a gamble for one friend to tell the other that they were attracted to them.

"What if I told you there were times you turned me on too?" I admitted.

Except Griffin didn't hear me.

His breathing was deep, and a soft snore escaped from between his lips.

"Oh, Griff." I pushed a lock of hair from his forehead and kissed his cheek. Then, I laid my head down on his chest and went to sleep.

The next morning, I was leaning over Griffin's counter, drinking my coffee and looking at my phone.

I had left Griffin sleeping and was trying to be quiet, so I didn't wake him.

About five minutes later, I was laughing at a meme when I heard the sound of feet shuffling from the direction of his door.

I looked over my shoulder. "Morning, sunshine."

Griffin stood there, naked and looking half-awake. He turned toward the direction of his bathroom. "I'll be right back."

"Okay. Coffee will be waiting for you."

He grunted in response.

I started watching a video, and while I heard the toilet flush and the sink run, I missed the sound of Griffin walking up behind me until his hands landed on my hips.

"Whoa." I jumped.

He kissed my shoulder. "Morning."

"Morning."

"Lean over again."

"Okay?" I agreed but didn't understand why.

He flipped up the back of the T-shirt I had stolen from him. "I was hoping you were naked under this."

He tapped the inside of my legs, so I spread them.

He rubbed the seam of my pussy. "We didn't have sex last night."

"You were tired."

"I'm never too tired for sex."

He pushed a finger inside me, and I hissed.

I hadn't been expecting the foreplay, and I wasn't quite wet enough.

"You okay?"

"Yeah. Just go slow."

Griffin continued to play with me until I was nice and wet.

" 'Go slow,' she says. But she's already soaking, and it's been less than two minutes."

He pushed down on my G-spot when he added another finger, and I moaned.

Soon, his hands were gone, and I heard the sound of the condom wrapper.

Both of us had gotten tested and come back clean, but we'd both decided it was best to keep using protection since we weren't technically in a committed relationship.

Griffin's cock replaced his fingers as he slowly thrust into me.

I pounded my fist on the counter. "So good."

He withdrew and pushed back in. He did this over and over, taking his time with me.

I was close to a climax, but I needed a little something more to push me over the edge.

I'd been letting him run the show so far, but now, I decided to push my hips back into him. Simply to let him know I wanted harder and faster.

But I wasn't expecting the slap across my ass.

I gasped in shock and excitement as I froze.

Griffin grabbed my hips and began pounding into me. Hard and fast, just like I wanted.

"Oh God," I yelled as I tried to find something to hold on to. I ended up finding the center of the sink and clutching my fingers tightly on to it as I held on for the ride.

Griffin tilted my hips, and his dick hit me right where I needed him. It wasn't but three deep thrusts, and my knees were buckling underneath me as an orgasm washed over me.

Grabbing my hips, Griffin kept me from falling as he slammed into me. With one last lunge, he exploded.

He collapsed on my back, breathing hard. He kissed the top of my back and stood. After he slid out of me, he helped me stand up and turn around.

After throwing the condom in the garbage, he pulled me into his arms. "That's a better way to wake up than any coffee."

I laughed and hugged him back.

TWENTY-SIX

GRIFFIN

AFTER MADELINE LEFT, I worked out, showered, and went over to my parents'. Sometimes, I didn't go over to their place on my day off, but I did often. Especially during football season. My dad and I had been watching football together since before I could remember.

"Here you go," my mom said, setting down some chips and dip on the coffee table for us.

"Thanks, Mom. I could have gotten those."

It didn't hurt that my mom liked to feed my father, too, and always kept snacks on hand.

"I was cleaning out the cupboards anyway."

"Right," I said.

She always made an excuse to bring food out to us. My father was spoiled, but it was a good thing he didn't act like it. She liked to take care of him but wouldn't be treated like a doormat.

"I pumped up the tires in her car this morning," he told me after Mom left the room.

I smiled and picked up a chip. "It's okay, Dad. I know how you two take care of each other."

My dad scooted to the end of his recliner and grabbed his own chip as a commercial came on the TV. "How's Madeline?"

I frowned. My dad didn't normally ask me this. Did he have some sort of dad Spidey sense?

"Uh, she's fine. I saw her this morning. She didn't mention anything. Is something going on with her parents?" It was the only thing I could think of since our parents were neighbors.

My father looked confused. "No, I was talking about how your mom kind of gave her the third degree last week."

Now, it was my time to look confused.

"Oh. She didn't tell you?"

I shook my head.

Dad looked around the corner, as if to make sure Mom couldn't hear what he was about to say. "Your mom was very surprised by the extravagant gift you got Madeline, and it worried her. She told Madeline that she worried you might not find someone because Madeline was in your life."

"Wow."

"She realized later that she'd overreacted. Madeline has never stopped you from dating, but it was too late. She's worried she offended her. But Madeline didn't say anything to you?"

I shook my head. "No."

"Look on the bright side, son. Maybe that means Madeline didn't make a big deal out of it, and that's why she didn't say anything to you."

"Yeah, that's probably it."

My dad patted my knee. "I'm sure it is. I've known Madeline since she was little. She's a good egg."

"Thanks, Dad."

I fiddled with the chip in my hand, thinking about what Dad had just told me. It was odd that she hadn't mentioned anything to me.

"Something else on your mind, Griffin?"

The commercials ended.

"Nah. The game's back on."

"Believe it or not, I can watch and listen at the same time. I'm not that old."

"I know, Dad."

"So, what's eating at you?"

My dad and I were close, and besides the one talk he'd given me about the birds and the bees a couple years too late, we didn't really talk about sex. I talked about women I dated, but we avoided bedroom stuff.

But if I trusted anyone, I trusted my father. More than Blake—that was for sure. And even more than Caleb, who was definitely more knowledgeable than Blake.

"I'm worried that Madeline didn't tell me about her conversation with Mom for a different reason."

"What would that be?"

I finally dunked my chip in the dip, so I had a reason to avoid my dad's eyes. "We kind of started sleeping together."

I popped the chip in my mouth and waited for a response, but my father was silent.

After swallowing, I looked over to see my dad watching the game.

I frowned. "Did you even hear what I said?" I asked.

My dad smiled.

Of course he had heard me.

His eyes left the television. "I heard you. I was waiting for you to stop freaking out about admitting what you told me."

"I'm not freaking out."

"You sure?"

"Yes."

"Okay. Good. Then, we can talk about this. So, why do you think Madeline didn't say anything?"

"Now that we're sleeping with each other, it has kind of limited either of us dating someone else." Although, to be fair, one week ago, we'd only spent one night together. It was possible I had misunderstood Madeline completely.

"So, you two aren't dating?"

"No. We have made it pretty clear that we're friends, having fun."

"And is this what you want?"

"Yes." *I think.* "What does that have to do with Mom and Mads?"

"Perhaps Madeline wants to be more than friends, and your mom made her feel guilty."

It was something to consider, but after the conversation we'd had in the dressing room yesterday, I didn't think it was true. "I don't know. She's never said she wants more. And she's had the opportunity."

"Hmm."

I sighed. "What does 'hmm' mean, Dad?"

His eyes widened. "Nothing. It's just a *hmm*. I'm simply thinking."

I looked down. "Do you think I made a mistake?"

"I can't tell you that, son. Does she make you happy? Do you like being with her?"

I looked at my dad. "Yes, but that's always been true, or she wouldn't be my closest friend."

"Okay, then how do you feel about no longer sleeping with her? How would you feel if she started dating someone else?" He lifted a hand. "You don't have to answer me. This is just something I want you to think about. And maybe you don't know, and that's okay. But when you do know, maybe you should make some decisions about where to take your friendship."

I nodded as I sat back on the couch and thought through my dad's questions.

I would be disappointed if we weren't sleeping together anymore. Sex with Madeline was better than with anyone else. And as far as her dating anyone else, I didn't like the idea, but it didn't make me jealous. Harris standing in Madeline's living room flashed across my brain.

Harris was different. He was a dipshit who didn't deserve her. I hadn't been jealous.

"You okay over there?" Dad asked.

"Yeah. Just thinking."

"Don't think too hard, or you'll miss the game."

This was my dad's way of telling me not to stress myself out. "Thanks, Dad."

"You're welcome, son."

TWENTY-SEVEN
MADELINE

I HIT play on my remote and grabbed the popcorn bowl.

After leaving Griffin's, I had come home and done some cleaning around my house. Then, I'd cooked myself a healthy dinner, and my reward was sweats, popcorn, and Netflix. I had slowly been binge-watching an older TV show with several seasons, and I was excited to see what happened next since I hadn't been able to watch for several days.

I was only about ten minutes into my first episode when there was a knock at my door.

I groaned and reluctantly got off my couch. Turning on the porch light, I looked through the small window in my front door to see Griffin standing on my steps.

I unlocked the door and opened it. "Did I miss a message from you?" I asked.

"No. I didn't tell you I was coming over," he said as he stepped inside. "It was a last-minute thing."

"Okay." I shut the door behind him. "What's up?"

Griffin took off his coat, threw it in the corner, and headed for my couch. "Whatcha watching?"

I sat down beside him. "Netflix."

"Do you mind if I watch with you?"

"No. But you're going to have to make more popcorn when we run out."

He smiled. "Deal."

I hit play, and we settled in.

After three bags of microwave popcorn and two episodes, I hit stop before the next one could start.

"Okay, spill it," I said.

"Spill what?" Griffin looked pretty clueless, except I knew him well enough to know he was hiding something.

"Spill why you're here. You didn't come over out of the blue for no reason."

He wiggled his eyebrows at me and ran a hand up my leg. "Maybe I came over to get you naked."

I made a buzzer noise. "Wrong answer. You were on edge when you got here. What happened? I thought you were with your parents today."

He groaned. "I was. My dad told me what my mom said to you last week. I felt a little foolish because I had no idea what he was talking about."

I winced. "Sorry. I didn't mean for you to be embarrassed."

"What did my mom say to you?"

I sighed and pressed myself deeper into the couch. "She knows you're lucky to have me, but she's worried that maybe I'm the reason you haven't settled down with anyone."

He shook his head. "She had no right to say that to you."

I lifted a shoulder. "She's just worried about her only child. And I think she really wants to have grandchildren."

159

"At this point, she'd probably be happy if I just knocked somebody up. She wants grandchildren more than she wants me to get married."

I poked him with my toe. "That's not true. She loves you and wants you to be happy."

"She still had no right to accuse you of being the reason I'm not in a serious relationship. Jeez."

"She didn't accuse me exactly. She wasn't saying I had done it on purpose. More like I was the unconscious reason."

"It still doesn't make it better."

"You didn't say anything to her, did you?"

"No. I wanted to talk to you first."

"Please don't. I don't want her to think I went to you and complained."

"Don't worry. I'll make sure and tell her that my dad was the one with the big mouth."

I laughed. "Poor Glen."

"Glen can take care of himself."

I chuckled for a few more seconds but lost my smile. "Seriously though, Griff. If your mom had asked that question a month ago, I would have laughed it off, but now, I do worry she has a point."

His brow furrowed. "How so?"

"We're sleeping together. And we're friends. We're not just a couple of people who hook up every once in a while. We see each other all the time. We talk all the time. And now, we can add that we sleep together all the time."

Griffin grinned. "Yeah, we can."

"Get your head out of the gutter. I'm being serious."

He tried to wipe his smile away, but the corners of his mouth were fighting him.

"What happens if the woman of your dreams walks into the bar one day, but you feel like you can't flirt because of me?"

"Okay. What happens if you bump into the man of your dreams at the grocery store?"

"Exactly. That's my point."

Griffin seemed to think this over before looking back at me. "And what is your suggestion?"

"Who says I have one?"

"Don't you?"

"Okay, I do. But I haven't been planning this. It only just came to me."

"What's your idea?"

"We keep sleeping together as long as we both benefit from the situation. If either of us wants to call it quits, whether it be because we met someone else or because we just don't want to do it anymore, the other person has to accept the reason, be understanding, and accept the quitter's wishes without a forced discussion at that time. There will be no fighting and no dragging it out." I tilted my head back and forth. "Maybe after a little time has passed, we can talk what happened, but I think in the moment, we both might be too close to our arrangement to be objective."

Griffin didn't say anything.

"What do you think?"

"So, if you meet someone or you're just plain tired of sleeping with me, you can say, *It's over, Griff*, and I'll have to accept it. Later, I can come to you and ask why you kicked me to the curb, but at the time, I can't press you for answers?"

"Yes, exactly. I figure there is less of a chance of feelings getting hurt if we have a cooling-off period before we talk about what happened."

He nodded his head. "Okay. That works for me."

I held out my hand. "Shall we shake on it and watch another episode?"

He grabbed my hand and pulled me into his lap. "I say, we fuck on it. Screw another episode."

"Oh, Griff, you have a way with words," I said sarcastically. "I think you already met the woman of your dreams, but she got scared away by your potty mouth."

He smiled. "I guess it wasn't meant to be. Unlike you and me and naked time. I'm absolutely convinced that this is meant to be."

I threw my arms around his neck. "Fuckshake it is then."

"What the hell is a fuckshake?"

"Instead of a handshake. It's a fuckshake."

Griffin laughed. "I agree. Fuckshake it is."

TWENTY-EIGHT

MADELINE

I WALKED into My Favorite Place and pounded my boots against the floor to get all of the snow off of them. Winter could be beautiful in Minnesota. As long as you didn't have to drive or walk outside in it. As far as I was concerned, it could snow the week of Christmas and then go away before the new year. That would be perfection.

After I wiped the bottom of my feet as well as I could, I stepped off the big rug by the front door and took a seat at the bar.

"Hey, Madeline," Casey said. "What can I get you?"

"Right now, I need a water."

"Boring but okay."

I laughed and looked around. "Where's Griff?"

She pointed to the back. "He's in his office, interviewing someone."

"Oh, that's right. He wants to find another bartender. How long have they been in there? A long time?"

She shook her head. "About fifteen minutes. But that's longer than the last guy. His interview was nine minutes."

"Wow. I guess Griffin is lucky to have found you and Mitch."

"He sure is. It's also a bad time of year to hire. Summer is when all the college kids come home."

"You're right, but college kids don't always stay. It might take more time, but at least he might find someone for the long haul." I looked toward the back, but the office door was still closed. "I told him to wait until after Thanksgiving, when people need extra cash for Christmas presents. But I suppose he'd be in the same shape as college kids who leave."

Casey shrugged. "I guess we'll see."

A few minutes later, Griffin's door opened, and he exited with a guy who looked to be in his mid-twenties. Griffin walked the guy to the door. "I'll keep you posted," he said, but as soon as the door shut behind him, he lost his smile. He came around the bar. "I will not be keeping him posted."

"That bad, huh?"

Griffin sighed. "No experience and wants to work only day shifts. First, we aren't that big of a place, and I specifically said in the posting that I am looking for someone to work nights and weekends."

"I don't get it," Casey said. "That's where you make all your money too. Griffin's day regulars don't tip worth a shit."

"Casey."

"I'm kidding. I know you have a soft spot for some of those old guys."

"No, you're right. They don't tip well. You make a lot more money working nights than days."

"Are you going to miss all those tips if you stop working so many nights?" I asked him.

He smiled at me. "Nah. I have something even better than money."

He meant sex. And me.

It had been over a month since my birthday, and Griffin and I still had our arrangement going on. Neither of us had met the person of our dreams so far, and neither one of us wanted to stop sleeping with the other.

Quite the opposite. Griffin and I spent almost every night together. I was getting more sex now than when I'd had a real boyfriend.

But Griffin had realized he was getting tired of the late nights all the time, so he'd decided he could afford to hire someone else, and then he could go to bed earlier on more nights.

"What's better than money?" Casey asked.

"Sleep," I said.

She shook her head. "You two aren't that old," she said and walked away.

"What the hell? I'm not old."

Griffin smiled. "You do have eight years on her."

"I'm still not old," I yelled loud enough for Casey to hear me.

She turned around. "You are when you pick sleep over money."

"Griffin, I'm sorry, but you'll need to find two new bartenders. Casey's ass needs to go."

He leaned on the bar, so we were face-to-face. "I'm not firing my best bartender because she called us old."

"Then, take it out of her Christmas bonus."

"I don't give them a Christmas bonus."

"You are a horrible boss. Casey should quit for that reason alone."

Griffin laughed. "Someone is feisty today. First, I should fire her, but now, you're on her side, and she should quit."

I frowned. "I just got my period, so that means no sexy times tonight."

"That's okay, babe. You and I went years without having sex. A couple nights won't kill us. Besides, you know your period doesn't bother me."

"I know," I said in a pouty voice. I was always crampy the first few days, which was the main reason we refrained from having sex.

I sat back in my seat and looked up at his daily sign.

WHAT IS YOUR FAVORITE THANKSGIVING SIDE DISH?

"Are you still going to your aunt's on Thanksgiving?" I asked. The holiday was three days away.

"Yep. Your mom still hosting?"

"Yes. Are we still planning to leave our Thanksgiving get-togethers early and spend the night together?"

He grinned. "Yes."

"Good, but not until I get some cheesy hash browns and scalloped corn."

"Cheesy hash browns and scalloped corn, huh?"

I pointed to his sign. "They're my favorite side dishes. I don't think we've ever spent Thanksgiving together. What's yours?"

"Mashed potatoes and pumpkin pie."

"Pumpkin pie is dessert."

"Not for me. I have a piece with dinner and then another for dessert."

"Your mother spoils you rotten. No wonder you can't find a woman."

He laughed and met my eyes. "Nah. Right now, I just don't want to."

TWENTY-NINE
GRIFFIN

I SAT BACK in my chair and rubbed my stomach. "The food was excellent, as always. I don't think I could eat another bite," I said.

"Thank you, Griffin," my aunt Ophelia said.

"Now, how about dessert?" I joked.

Everyone at the table groaned. I was pretty sure they were all as full as I was.

"Let's give everyone a half hour or so," Ophelia said. "Then, we'll break out the pie."

I looked at my watch. It was already after two in the afternoon, and I had plans to meet Madeline at her house by four.

I pushed my chair back and stood. "I'll help with dishes."

My mom's jaw dropped. "Are you feeling okay?"

I chuckled. "Why do you ask?"

"Because I usually have to pull your teeth to get you to help. You always run off and watch football with your dad."

I shrugged. "Shame on me then. I should help more."

My mom shook her head as she stood. "My son has been replaced by a robot," she muttered as she carried her own plate to the kitchen.

I picked up as many plates as I could and followed her.

An hour and a half later, we had finished dessert, and I was itching to leave. I was trying to get into the game, but four o'clock was inching closer, and my aunt lived about forty-five minutes from Madeline. I was already going to be late, but I was starting to feel bad about leaving. I hadn't skipped out on Thanksgiving since high school.

"Griffin, if you want to leave, then leave," my dad said out of nowhere.

"What?"

"It's obvious you want to go, son."

"Will Mom be upset?"

My father laughed. "You're a thirty-year-old man. Your mom will be fine. Especially if you tell her you're leaving early to see a woman."

"But that's not—" Well, it was kind of true. "I don't want to lie."

"You're going to see Madeline, right?"

"Yes."

"And is she a woman?"

I smiled. She most certainly was. "Yes."

"Then, it's not a lie."

I shook my head and laughed. "You know Mom is going to think other things, so it's kind of a lie." Then, I threw my arm around my dad. "But thanks for the support."

He hugged me back. "You're welcome. Now, get out of here."

I went to find my mom. "Hey, Mom. I gotta go." I looked at my aunt. "Thanks for everything."

"You're welcome."

"Where are you going?" Mom asked.

"I'm going to meet someone."

"Griffin, aren't you a little old to be leaving early on Thanksgiving to go and get drunk with your friends?"

"Mom, I haven't done something like that in years. I'm not going to meet my friends." I thought about my dad's advice. "I'm going to meet a woman, okay?"

My mom's eyes lit up. "You are? Who?"

"I'm not telling you. It's still new. Don't get too excited, okay?"

She nodded way too enthusiastically. "Okay." She pulled me into a hug. "Have fun. Tell this woman hi for me."

I kissed her cheek. "Bye, Mom."

She reluctantly let me go, and I hightailed it out of the kitchen before she could ask more questions.

"Bye, Dad," I said on my way out.

He smiled at me. "Bye, son."

And with that, I was off to Madeline's.

I was late, but I had already texted Madeline, so she knew I hadn't ditched her. She greeted me at the door with a huge mug.

"What's this?"

"Spiked hot cocoa."

I grinned. I also saw that she had the gas fireplace running and a Christmas movie pulled up on the television.

"Someone's ready for the holidays, huh?"

"Always. You know Christmas is my favorite time of year."

"That I do."

She grabbed my hand and led me over to the couch. "I thought we could take turns picking movies to watch while we get drunk on peppermint schnapps."

"I'm game. You know I'm picking *Die Hard* though, right?"

"I would never expect anything less," she told me.

Madeline grabbed a blanket and threw it over our laps, and she cuddled up next to me as I put my arm around her.

"Are you ready for me to hit play?" she asked.

"Go for it. What are we watching again?"

We hadn't had sex since Sunday, and I knew she was almost done with her cycle. If I kissed her, I had a strong feeling she'd melt into me and ask me to take her to the bedroom.

But I didn't want that. I was more than content to snuggle with her on her couch and watch movies.

"A new Netflix movie. If it's not good, I'll turn it off. But the preview looked cute."

I kissed her on the head. "Works for me." I was simply happy to be with her. "I have to warn you, I ate a lot of food, and there's a chance I might fall asleep."

She patted my stomach. "That's okay. You sleep today because we have a big day ahead of us tomorrow."

"What's going on tomorrow? I thought we'd planned to

hole ourselves up here and not do anything until I have to work tomorrow night."

"We're putting up the Christmas tree." She grinned up at me.

I groaned playfully. "I should have known."

"If you do a good job, I'll have a present for you later."

"Are you bribing me with sex, babe?"

She laughed. "No. I got you your very own homemade pumpkin pie."

"You should have led with that. I'd do almost anything for pumpkin pie."

THIRTY

GRIFFIN

THE FOLLOWING Monday was like usual, except when I looked outside, the street was decorated for the holidays.

Bar traffic during this time of year was unlike any other. Some of my regulars were too busy to stop in as much as they normally did. Meanwhile, there were people who hated the holidays and came in to drink more than usual.

I was looking at a pretty good crowd for the early afternoon in the beginning of the week when my phone rang.

I could see on my watch that it was my mom, but I was in the middle of pouring a drink with another customer waiting. I would just call her back.

But when my phone rang again, right after my mom hung up, I knew something wasn't right. My mother did not call multiple times in a row. I couldn't put this off for later.

I turned to my bartender. "Mitch, I need you to call Casey and see if she can come in." I had a feeling I was going to need to take off as soon as I answered this call.

His eyebrows furrowed. "Is something wrong?"

"I'm not sure yet. Can you please call her? If she doesn't

answer, call someone else to come in." I didn't wait for Mitch to answer; I just ran toward my office.

I had missed my mom's second call, too, so I quickly dialed her back.

The phone clicked, and I heard crying.

"Mom?" My heart was racing in my chest, and I broke out into a cold sweat.

"Oh, Griffin. I need you to..." Her voice dropped too low for me to hear.

"Mom, I need you to repeat that."

Silence.

"*Mom.*"

"Mr. Davis?" a deep, masculine voice said.

"Yes? What is going on?"

"This is Dr. Long. Your father had a heart attack."

I fell against the wall as if my legs could no longer hold me up. "Is he—is he okay?"

"Your father is alive at this time. But I think it's best you come to the hospital right away."

I closed my eyes and fought off panic because I didn't have time for it. I took a deep breath, opened my eyes, and stood up.

"What hospital?"

"Southdale."

"Tell my mom I'm on my way."

My arrival to the hospital was a blur. I barely remembered leaving the bar, and the next thing I knew, I was asking someone at a desk where Glen Davis was.

My father was still in the emergency department when I got to the hospital, and my mom jumped up from her chair when she saw me in the doorway of my dad's room.

She rushed toward me.

"Mom, shouldn't Dad be in the ICU or something like that? There's no way they can send him home today."

My mom cupped my face. "Oh, honey. They don't think your father is going to make it. I was worried you wouldn't get here in time to say good-bye."

I stepped back and pushed her hands off me. "No. No way. Dad is healthy." I shook my head. "I don't believe you."

My mom moved toward me again and grabbed my hands. "Shh. It's okay, Griffin. Why don't you just go in and talk to him. Okay?"

I nodded even though I was mad at her for telling me that my dad was going to die. I approached the bed and sat in the chair my mom had just vacated.

He was surrounded by machines, and his face was pale. He looked like someone who had put on a mask of my dad. And when I picked up his hand, it was cold.

"Dad, please wake up."

The last time I had seen him was Thanksgiving. He'd seemed fine. I didn't understand what had happened.

"I'm sorry I left early. I should have stayed with you."

I didn't even know I had been crying until I tasted the tears on my mouth.

"I don't want to lose you." I squeezed his hand. "Please, you have to get better. Who am I going to get advice from if you leave?" I joked, but my father didn't move. And he didn't squeeze my hand back.

I didn't know how long my mother had left me alone to talk to my dad, but she came back after some time.

"What happened?" I asked her.

She shrugged. "I only know what the doctor and nurses told me. He was at work in the back of the warehouse, and someone found him unconscious. They called 911 and brought him here."

"He wasn't complaining of any chest pain?" I asked.

"No."

"No complaints about anything?" I found it hard to believe there hadn't been any signs.

"Griffin, honey, if he had any symptoms, he didn't share them with me."

I looked at my father. "Why wouldn't you have said anything?" I asked him. "Someone might have been able to help you sooner."

"I understand you're upset, Griff. I am too."

I looked up at my mom as she took my dad's other hand, and I felt bad for getting mad. Yes, he was my father, but he was her husband. And I knew my mom loved him. I didn't know what she would do without him.

"I'm sorry, Mom."

"For what?"

"For getting mad. I had no right."

"It's fine. You didn't mean it."

I hung my head in shame and nodded. When I looked up, she had his hand against her face.

"Jeez, Mom, come and sit over here."

"No, no. I'm fine."

"You sure?"

"Yes."

I scanned the hall. "Why hasn't anyone come in to check on him?" I looked at the monitor. I wasn't a doctor and didn't know what everything meant, but I could see that his heart was still beating. "Shouldn't they be moving him somewhere else by now?"

My mom looked at me, her eyes full of tears. "Honey, the doctor said your dad has already coded four times. He said his heart can't take much more."

"Can't they do surgery or something?" I heard all the time about people getting triple bypass surgery. I'd even heard of a quadruple bypass.

She shook her head. "He needs to be stable before they can take him to surgery. And so far, they haven't been able to get him stable."

I studied my dad once more. "He looks pretty stable to me."

And the second I said those words, the monitor flatlined and started to beep.

THIRTY-ONE
MADELINE

I LEFT THE CONFERENCE ROOM, ready to call it a day.

I hated Mondays. Every second dragged on, especially when the entire afternoon was meetings.

Sometimes, I wondered how they expected us to do our actual jobs when they put us in meetings all day.

When I got to my desk, the first thing I did was pick up my phone. I was shocked to see I had missed several calls.

Griffin had called me, followed by his mom and my mom.

I didn't even wait to call anyone back. I grabbed my coat and purse and told my boss I had to leave early.

I called Griffin first as I walked to my car, but he didn't answer, so I sent him a text before I left the parking lot.

I was just about to call him a second time when my phone rang. It was my mom again.

"Hello?"

"Honey, have you spoken to Griffin?"

"No. I tried to call him, but he didn't answer. I've been

in meetings all afternoon, and they won't let us take our phones in."

"Oh, honey."

"Mom, what is wrong? I saw his mom had called too."

"Madeline, Griffin's dad died of a heart attack this afternoon."

I sucked in a breath and slammed a hand over my mouth.

"Camile called me earlier to see if I knew where you were. Apparently, Griffin left the hospital, and his mom is worried about him."

I was already crying, and it took me a second to steady my voice. "I'm on my way to his place right now. Since I'm driving, would you mind letting Camile know that I'm checking on him?"

"Of course, honey. I'll call her right away."

"Thank you."

When I got to the bar, I went in through the back way. It had occurred to me to stop and talk to Griffin's staff to see if anyone had seen him, but I would only do that if I couldn't find him in his apartment.

I knocked when I got upstairs, but he didn't answer, so I tried the door, and it was unlocked.

I slowly pushed the door open, wondering what I would find but I didn't see anything. Griffin's shades were drawn, and since it was winter, the sun was almost set, so the space was dark.

I gently closed the door, slipped off my shoes, and padded to the bedroom. It was just as dark in there, but I could see Griffin's figure facing away from me on the bed.

I breathed a sigh of relief and sent a group text to my

mom and Camile to let them know that Griffin was at home and safe. Then, I set my phone on his dresser and slipped into bed behind him.

I hesitantly put my hand on his back. "Griffin, I'm so sorry. I just want you to know that I'm here if you need me."

Griffin slowly rolled over, pushed his face into my chest, and silently cried.

Sometime later, I woke with a start, unsure of why my body was on high alert.

And then I remembered.

Glen, Griffin's dad, had died.

I had let Griffin cry on me for some time while I stroked his hair, and we must have fallen asleep. I had no idea what time it was. The only clue as to how late it might be was how hungry I was.

Griffin stirred beside me, his face still buried in my shoulder, and I froze. I honestly didn't know what to do for him, and I didn't want to mess anything up.

He lifted his head until we lay face-to-face on the pillow. Since I felt like there were no words, I put my hand on his cheek to let him know I cared.

The last thing I expected was for him to kiss me. Or for that kiss to explode into an urgency I had never experienced before with him.

As if we were on borrowed time, Griffin practically ripped off all our clothes until we were both naked. I felt like his hands had multiplied as he touched me everywhere. I didn't know if he needed to feel that I was alive or if he wanted to make sure I was really there.

I understood that this was a reaction to his dad's death. I understood that he needed to feel life and that this was his way of coping.

So, when he rolled me onto my back, I spread my legs and let him push his way inside.

He hadn't spoken a single word to me since I had gotten here, but I ran my hands over his back and shoulders and told him to take what he needed from me. That I was there for him.

I only wanted to make sure he felt good.

But I should have known Griffin wouldn't let things go down that way. He rode me hard, as if every pump of his hips was a way to exorcise his grief, but he didn't use me the way he could have.

Every thrust was aimed right for my G-spot. After sleeping together for a month, he knew exactly how to reach it and how to make me feel good. And tonight was no exception.

I felt guilty, getting so much pleasure from Griffin when his father would never feel anything again, but he didn't let up, and I knew I was going to be sore tomorrow.

When I lost the fight between desire and remorse, desire won. And as I cried out in pleasure, Griffin slammed home and poured himself into me.

We were both breathing hard and shaking when he lifted his head and looked down on me.

We had both barely regained our breath when he kissed me, and he grew hard inside me again.

Griffin grunted and began to thrust.

THIRTY-TWO

MADELINE

THE NEXT MORNING, I pulled myself from Griffin's bed, feeling drained and out of sorts. I grabbed sweats from his dresser and got dressed before shuffling my way to the kitchen in search of food. Any kind of food. I was so hungry; I didn't even care if I made noise and woke Griffin up.

Last night had been a whirlwind of sex, sleep, and more sex, and I'd never gotten a chance to eat. I had known my best friend was suffering, but I'd had no idea that he would refuse to talk about anything. Instead, every time he woke up and I tried to comfort him, he would pull me into his arms and make love to me.

Now, not only was I starving, but I was also thirsty, and my vagina was sore and wet. We hadn't used protection once last night. I blamed it on the grief, and since we had both already been tested, it wasn't something I was going to bring up with him. He already had enough on his plate.

I grabbed a glass from the cupboard, filled it with water, and downed the whole thing. As I set the empty glass down,

I spotted a banana in the corner and practically attacked it as I shoved huge bites in my mouth. I never knew a banana could taste so good.

Feeling a tad more human, I poured a bowl of cereal and took some time with scarfing that down. Only after that did I feel more like I could think. I had to figure out what I needed to do today.

First things first. I needed to let work know I wasn't coming in and go home to get some clothes. I should also probably find out if there was anything I could do to help Griffin's mom.

I called work to tell them that someone close to me had died. I had to take vacation time since Glen wasn't a family member, but it was worth it if it meant I could be there for my best friend.

I was just hanging up when Griffin came out of his bedroom in sweatpants, looking awful. His skin was pale, and he had bags under his eyes. My heart went out to him.

"Hey," I said. "Can I get you something to eat?" I stood up from the stool at his counter. "Or coffee. Sorry, I haven't made any yet."

He put his hand on mine as he sat down. "Madeline, you don't have to baby me. I can make my own coffee."

"It's no trouble. You know I'll drink it too."

He lifted his hand. "Go ahead."

I got the coffee started and came around to him. Something told me that I needed to approach Griffin with caution. Maybe it was last night. The only real emotion he'd shown was when he cried on my shoulder.

"How are you feeling?"

He shot me a look.

"Stupid question. I'm sorry." *Think, Madeline. Think.* "Is there anything you need me to do today? I already called into work, so I'm free to help out wherever I can."

He sighed. "I wish you hadn't done that."

"Too late. I'm not going anywhere."

"Even if I make you leave?" he said with a scowl.

I nearly took a step back. Griffin was never mean to me, but his comment had almost hurt my feelings. I took a second to remind myself that he was heartbroken, and when people were in pain, they often lashed out at the ones they loved the most. And that included best friends.

I squared my shoulders. "You can try, but I'll just come back like a bad rash."

The corner of his mouth tilted up for a second, and I took that as a good sign.

"Your mom is probably going to need help today. Do you want me to take care of the bar? Do you want me to close it for the day? I can call your employees and put out a closed sign."

He dropped his forehead in his hand. "Shit. I don't know what to do. I should close the bar for a few days, but I don't know if my mom needs help paying for the…" He swallowed. "For the funeral."

I remembered when my grandfather had died and my parents spoke in low tones, so my grandmother and I wouldn't hear. I knew funerals weren't cheap.

"How about you let me help with the bar? I don't know everything you do, but I can probably wing it for a few days. And we'll close on the day of your father's funeral, so you don't have to worry about any emergencies."

"Thank you," he said without meeting my eyes.

I wasn't sure if he was going to cry again, and I also knew that if he did, he would probably be embarrassed in the light of day.

I put my arms around him, and he buried his nose between my breasts. "You're welcome, but you don't have to thank me. I am your best and longest friend. I hope you know I'd do just about anything for you."

I thought I had gone too sentimental for him, but he raised his head until he reached my neck, where he started kissing me.

I closed my eyes and leaned into him.

No man could make me lose concentration like Griffin, but it was a good thing the rest of my body said no. When he put his hand between my legs, I winced and stepped back.

I shook my head. "No."

His eyebrows flew up. "No?"

"No."

"I don't think you've ever said no to me before."

"We've never had so much sex before. I'm sore."

He frowned and looked down. "Oh. I'm sorry."

I lifted his chin. "Don't be sorry. I didn't say no to anything last night." I smiled to reassure him. "But right now, my vagina can't handle any more sex." I looked down at his pants to see him hard and shook my head in amazement. "Frankly, I am shocked to see you can get it up."

He smiled.

"Just give the poor girl a day or so, and then she'll be ready for you again." I ran my hand over his scruff. "I'm going to go home, shower, and get a change of clothes, and then I'll be back. Do you think you can give me a rundown of the business? I've seen you work, but I don't know every-thing you do."

"Sure."

"Do you need anything while I'm out? Do you want me to call anyone for you? Do you need me to check on your mom?"

He shook his head. "I'll call her in just a few." He turned his head away. "I just can't believe he's…"

I hugged him. "I know, baby. I know."

THIRTY-THREE
GRIFFIN

I STARED at my reflection as I straightened my tie. I had shaved today, but I still looked like I hadn't slept all week.

"Sorry, Dad, this is as good as I'm going to get."

I stepped back and took one last look before I left the room. I hadn't dressed up in forever, and I hated that the reason I was wearing a suit was because today was my father's funeral.

Madeline poked her head in my bedroom, wearing a conservative black dress. "Are you ready to go?" she asked.

I honestly didn't know what I would have done without her over the last few days. She had pretty much taken over running the bar for me while I helped my mom plan the funeral. I was lucky she could take time off work to help me run my business. I should tell her to add herself to the payroll because she deserved to be compensated.

"As ready as I'll ever be."

One would think after all the planning I had done this week, I'd be ready, but I wasn't.

The funeral went as well as could be expected. All my friends arrived to show their support, and even though it was a cold December day, the sun blazed high in the sky.

The gathering after the funeral and burial was at my parents' house, and I hated every second of it.

"I'm so sorry for your loss," the hundredth person today said to me.

I knew they didn't know what else to say, but I was sick of hearing it. My dad dying was way more than a "loss." He was my father, and he was gone forever.

I snuck out to the garage and turned on the heater to stay warm. I needed a little time away from all the well-meaning guests, but I felt bad about leaving my mom in there alone.

I was going through my father's tools when the door opened behind me. I quickly turned to see who had caught me skipping out. When I recognized Blake, I immediately relaxed.

"I thought you were my mother or my aunt coming out here to drag me back in."

"Nah," Blake said as he walked down the concrete stairs and over to me. He pulled out a flask from his suit jacket. "You look like you could use this."

I lifted the cap and took a long drink. The whiskey went down with ease.

"Thanks," I said, handing it back. I wasn't a huge drinker despite my choice of business, but sometimes, there was no substitute for alcohol.

Blake took a sip and gave it to me again.

"I probably shouldn't," I said.

"And you probably shouldn't be hiding out in the garage after your father's funeral."

"Good point." I took another drink. I tried to look inside. "There's not much left."

"Then, let's finish it up."

"If I get drunk, my mother is going to kill me."

Blake scoffed. "You're not going to get drunk. But if you're lucky, you might get a much-needed buzz."

MADELINE

I watched as Griffin and Blake came in from the garage, laughing.

I groaned and rushed over to them before all the guests saw them. I stopped them both with hands to their chests. "Gentlemen, I would like to remind you that you are at a funeral reception, and many would not appreciate your humor."

They both tried to school their faces, but they couldn't stop snickering.

I leaned in closer to them. "Are you drunk?"

There wasn't any alcohol being served today, so I couldn't be sure.

"Blake brought a little something," Griffin said.

Blake put his hand on mine. "I would have saved you some if I had known you wanted to join us."

"No, thank you."

Griffin reached over and took my hand from Blake's. "I need to talk to you about something," he said to me.

I frowned. "Is something wrong?"

He seemed to think quite a bit about this. "No."

"Then, can it wait? Your mother has guests. *You* have guests. They're here to see both of you."

"Please. I don't want to hear one more person tell me they're sorry." He leaned down and whispered, "I think I might punch the next person who says it."

I could smell the alcohol on his breath. Maybe it was a good idea to take him somewhere and talk to him before he embarrassed himself and his mom.

"Let's go talk," I said. I studied Blake. "Are you going to be okay? You aren't going to do anything stupid, are you?"

He put his hand to his chest. "*Moi?*"

"Yeah, you."

"I can hold my liquor. I'll be on my best behavior."

I rolled my eyes. I doubted that, but Griffin was my main concern.

"Will you go find Caleb, please?" I asked Blake. Hopefully, Caleb would keep an eye on him.

I put my arm in Griffin's. "Let's go talk."

He led me down to his old bedroom. He stopped at the doorway and looked at his parents' bedroom door. He must have realized he was staring because he shook his head and walked into his bedroom.

I closed the door behind me. "Okay, what is it—"

Before I could finish, Griffin was kissing me.

My best friend had been very needy and overly sexual over the last week. I had been there for him when he needed me, but now wasn't the time.

I pulled away. "Griffin, did you have something you needed to talk to me about, or did you just want to come in here and have sex?"

He grinned. "I want to have sex."

I put my hand on his chest. "No."

"No again?"

"Griffin, I am not having sex with you here. The house is full of people mourning your father." I took a deep breath and dared to say the next words. "You should be mourning your father."

He lost his smile, and his face turned angry. "I don't want to mourn him. I want him here."

I picked up his hand. "I know you do, Griff, but—"

He yanked his hand away. "No, you don't. You don't know. Both of your parents are still alive."

I nodded and looked down at my hands. "You're right. Wrong choice of words."

"Forget it. I'm out of here."

I raised my head in time to see him throw open the bedroom door and march out of the room.

I followed him into the living room.

"Blake?" Griffin shouted.

Blake popped up. "What?"

"Let's go."

"All right."

Within seconds, the two of them walked out the front door.

Camile came up and stood beside me.

"He's grieving," I told her.

"I know." She turned and walked away.

Griffin didn't come back, and when I went to his apartment after the reception, he wasn't there either.

Not knowing what else to do, I reluctantly went home and texted him for the twentieth time.

I tried not to worry too much, but I was really scared for my best friend.

THIRTY-FOUR
MADELINE

MY PHONE RANG as I was leaving work, and I sighed when I saw Casey's number. Today was supposed to be a day I could go home and relax after work.

I'd been working double shifts for two weeks lately. I went to my job during the day and then over to the bar after work to take care of things.

Griffin hadn't been around much, and when he was, he often drank with the customers. I had never seen him do that before, and now, it seemed like he couldn't stop. Casey and Mitch and the other bartenders often had to kick him out and send him upstairs.

Thankfully, they were all understanding of what Griffin was going through and were loyal employees. And I had managed to hire someone the week of Glen's funeral. The new bartender had been training two weeks and was working tonight. Griffin had plans to be with Troy, which was why I was supposed to have the night off.

I was going to take a long soak in the tub and go to bed early.

"Hello?" I said, answering my phone.

"I am so sorry, Madeline, but I think you need to come down here."

I didn't even ask why because I assumed the answer wouldn't be good.

"I'll be there as soon as I can."

When I got to the bar, I found Griffin lying down in the circular booth—the same booth he had given me an orgasm in—with an ice pack over his eye.

"What happened?" I asked Casey.

"Nothing," Griffin said, slurring his word.

"I wasn't asking you," I said in a firm voice. I looked at Casey.

"He got in a fight with a customer."

"Shit," I said and rubbed my forehead. I was on the verge of a massive headache. "Where's the customer?"

"He left."

"Do you think he'll press charges?"

She shook her head. "Griffin was too drunk to even fight back. If anyone could press charges, it would be him."

"Don't be so sure about that. He can press charges all he wants. Making them stick is another thing."

"I doubt it. We explained that his father died, so Griffin is not himself."

"I hope you're right." I looked at Griffin. "Can you help me get him upstairs?"

"Yes," Casey said.

Griffin sat up. "I can get up on my own." He pushed himself out of his seat and only wobbled a little bit. "I don't need anyone to help me."

I gestured to the back of the bar. "Lead the way then."

Going up the stairs after a drunk person who refused help was a long and painful process. I wanted to smack some sense into him, but in his state, it would be pointless.

Finally, after what felt like a year, we made it inside, and Griffin collapsed on his couch.

I sat down on his coffee table. "Griffin, what is going on?"

I thought maybe he'd talk to me with alcohol in his system because he sure wouldn't talk to me while he was sober. Although those times were becoming rarer and rarer.

"What do you mean?" he asked, pulling his ice pack away and looking at it.

I ripped it from his hand and threw it down next to me.

"Whoa," he said. "You're mad."

"Hell yes, I'm mad. I've been busting my ass, trying to keep your bar running, all while working forty hours a week at my own job. Meanwhile, you're drinking and getting into fights."

He held up a finger. "One. One fight."

"Oh," I said sarcastically. "That makes it so much better."

"I think it does."

"I can't keep doing this."

He frowned. "Doing what?"

"I can't keep running things for you. I don't have the energy. I'm exhausted."

"No one said you had to."

"You're unbelievable."

"Okay," he said in a smart tone.

"I'm telling you I can't do this anymore, and you're telling me no one asked me to." I wanted to pull my hair out from frustration. "Griffin, I am your friend. Actually, at this point, I would like to think we're more than friends. You don't have to ask me. It's what friends do. But friends don't turn around and use their loved ones. You need to figure out what you want because I can't do everything for you any longer."

As I said my speech, I realized something. Something I couldn't believe I hadn't realized before.

"*Holy shit,*" I whispered.

"What?"

I looked at him in shock. "I love you, Griffin Davis. I love you more than just a best friend. I'm *in* love with you." I shook my head in disbelief. That explained why I'd been busting my ass for him.

He looked away from me. "I didn't ask for this from you."

Ouch. No, *I love you too.* Not even a *thank you.*

I picked up his hand. "You're right. But I do love you, and it is killing me to see you throw away everything you worked so hard for."

"You wouldn't understand."

"I don't know how you feel, but I do know that your father would be sad if he could see you now."

Griffin's head whipped back in my direction.

"Your dad would not want you to slowly kill yourself, drinking, while running your business into the ground. I want to help you, but I need you to help me. I just can't go one like I have. Not all by myself." I sent him a small smile. "Please."

He gently pulled his hand out from under mine, and I thought he was going to put it on top. I actually thought he was going to reassure me that he would clean up his act and be a better boss.

"Get out."

"Excuse me?" I said, taken aback.

"Get out, Madeline. I don't want or need your help."

"But, Griffin...I love you. I want to help."

He jumped up from the couch and pointed to the door. "I said, get out," he said through clenched teeth. "Now."

I sluggishly stood as I tried not to cry. "Please, Griff."

He marched over to his door and opened it. "Leave. I don't want to see you anymore."

I was taken aback. "Do you mean..."

"It's over."

"But why?"

"I don't have to tell you that. It's part of our deal, remember?"

Maybe he wasn't as drunk as I'd thought he was because he remembered the terms of our agreement.

I nodded. "Okay. I'll leave. But I know you'll regret this when you sober up," I said as I stepped outside his door.

"Don't count on it," he said and slammed the door in my face.

THIRTY-FIVE
GRIFFIN

"GET YOUR FUCKING ASS UP. NOW," someone yelled as they kicked my bed.

I turned my head and opened one eye. "Blake?"

"No. The fucking tooth fairy. Yes, it's Blake."

I slowly sat up. "What are you doing here?"

"Dragging your drunk ass out of bed."

"I'm not drunk."

Blake sighed. "I'm not sure if that's better or worse."

"What do you mean?"

"It's five o'clock in the evening, and you're still in bed." He eyed me. "When's the last time you drank?"

"Not since Madeline left."

"You mean, not since you broke her heart and kicked her out."

I winced. I felt bad about that, but things were better this way.

"So, you haven't been drinking every night while your friends and family bust their asses, keeping your bar afloat?"

"What are you talking about?"

"While you've been neglecting your bar, the people who care about you have been making sure you don't lose your business."

I rubbed my forehead. "I had no idea."

"And why would you? We haven't seen you in weeks."

I looked up. "Weeks? Madeline was just here a couple of days ago."

Blake got down on his haunches. "Griffin, it's been over a month since your dad died."

I hung my head in shame. "But I haven't gone grocery shopping or paid any bills." I didn't eat much, but I knew I had been eating every day.

"Your mom brings you food while you're sleeping. Or passed out. And we've been paying your bills."

I didn't like his accusation that I had been passed out. "I told you that I haven't been drinking."

"Sleeping then. Whatever." He shrugged. "Either way, something has to change."

I didn't want anything to change. I wanted things to go back to exactly the way they had been. My dad alive and my life back to normal.

Blake pulled out his phone and pointed to the date, shoving the phone into my line of sight. "It's January, man. You missed Christmas and New Year's. You left your widowed mom to spend Christmas alone."

"Oh my God." I broke out in a sweat and felt like I might puke.

"Not to mention, you pushed away one of the best women in the world. You're lucky she loves you enough to make sure someone is around to cover your ass."

Love. The word vibrated in my head until my ears rang.

"I love you, Griffin Davis. I love you more than just a best friend. I'm in love with you."

"Oh, fuck. I think I'm going to be sick."

Blake quickly dragged me off my bed and hauled me into the bathroom before I emptied the contents of my stomach into the toilet. After I was doing nothing but dry-heaving, Blake turned on the water in my shower and shoved me inside.

He handed me a toothbrush and toothpaste on the side of the curtain. "Scrub up and brush your teeth. We have somewhere to be."

"You're taking me to church? On a..." *Shit.* I didn't even know what day of the week it was.

"It's Thursday," Blake said.

"It doesn't matter if it's Sunday; you are the last person I thought would bring me to church."

"Just get out of the car."

I sighed and pushed open the door to get out.

I followed Blake through the back door of the church and down a flight of stairs into a room full of people sitting in a circle.

A middle-aged woman smiled and stood. "Good to see you, Blake. And I see you've brought a friend." She pointed to the wall. "Please, grab a chair and take a seat."

"Dude," I hissed in Blake's ear. It looked like an Alcoholics Anonymous meeting, but I was not an alcoholic. And I had seen Blake drink plenty of times. He was a hypocrite, bringing me to AA. "Why did you bring me here?"

He ignored me.

The leader of the group waved her hands out. "Group, can we make room for Blake and..." She looked at me.

"Griffin," I admitted.

"Hello, Griffin. I'm Lennon."

The group scooted their chairs around while Blake and I grabbed our own.

After we were all seated, Lennon said, "Would anyone like to start today?"

Blake put his hand up. "I'll go first."

I sat back in surprise and with some judgment. If he gave the group some spiel about being on the wagon, I was going to call bullshit. He was the one who had given me the flask at my father's funeral reception.

He stood and cleared his throat. "I'm Blake."

"Hi, Blake," the group said.

"It's been eleven years, three months, and twenty-one days since my mother died, and I still think about her every day."

My jaw dropped open.

"Just four years earlier, we had lost my grandma—my mom's mom—to breast cancer. They hadn't caught it until it was stage four." He smiled sadly. "Grandma was one of those women who refused to go to the doctor for anything, and so by the time my mom and my uncle could convince her, it was too late."

I'd known that his grandmother and mother had passed away years ago, but I'd had no idea it still affected him. I had been in college at the time. I had come home for his mother's funeral, but Blake and I never talked about it. Not once. I suddenly felt like a piece-of-shit friend for never asking.

He sighed. "So, two years later, when my mom was diagnosed, I didn't worry because they'd caught it early. But I was wrong. And this might sound bad, but to this day, I can't figure out if it was better to go fast like my grandma or slow like my mom." He looked down at his hands. "I guess it doesn't matter when you die from the same thing, huh?"

He looked over at me, and despite my guilt, I met his eyes.

"Anyway"—Blake turned his attention back to the group —"I did some stupid things, pushed some people away because I didn't want to get hurt again, and made a mess of my life for a while. I know everyone has to go through their own journey, but if I can help anyone who feels like I did eleven years ago, I have to try. Because you might regret throwing everything away. While I still miss my mom and would do just about anything to have her back, I know she wouldn't want me throwing away my future." He smiled one more time and sat.

Neither of us said anything to each other as we listened to others speak. There were people who had lost spouses and some who had lost children. There was even a couple who had lost close friends.

Not everyone talked. Some just listened. I liked that it felt like it was a safe space to connect with people who understood what I was going through.

When we circled the complete group and it got around to me, Lennon asked, "Would you like to share, Griffin?"

I shook my head, but then I stopped myself and stood up. "Hi, I'm Griffin."

"Hi, Griffin."

Even though I had known everyone was going to say hi back, it still kind of startled me, and I jumped a bit.

"I lost my dad a month ago. Heart attack. We hadn't even known he was sick." I was getting choked up, and I really didn't want to cry, so I paused and took a breath. "I miss him. I miss him a lot. But since this is all new to me, I'm still taking things one day at a time." I looked at Blake. "And I hope that it's not too late to keep some of the people that I pushed away."

He smiled at me and nodded once.

I didn't know what else to say, so I put my hand up awkwardly and said, "Thanks," before sitting down.

Blake slapped me on the shoulder, and I knew that was his guy way of giving me a hug.

THIRTY-SIX

MADELINE

I PULLED up to the church for Christina and Troy's wedding rehearsal, grabbed my dress and toiletries, and quickly ran inside. I'd been told to bring all of my stuff because, tomorrow, we were going to get dressed and do our hair and our makeup together as a group.

And while I was looking forward to Christina's big day, I hoped all the busywork and excitement would help keep me from worrying about Griffin. Of course, it would be hard to forget that he was the person I was supposed to be walking down the aisle with. Troy's cousin was Griffin's replacement. I could only hope that Troy's cousin was handsome and rich and would make me forget all about falling in love with my best friend.

The first person I saw when I got in the building was Hope.

"Remind me to never get married in the middle of winter," I said to her. "*Brr*. It's so cold."

"Tell me about it." She waved her hand. "Come on. I'll show you where you can put your stuff."

I followed her down the hall to a room with tables and mirrors lined up against the wall and a rack with other bridesmaid dresses hanging on it.

"You can put your things wherever. The pastor promised me that the room and the church will be locked tonight."

"I'm not too worried. If someone wants to steal used makeup and a bunch of bridesmaid dresses, then they have bigger problems than I do."

Hope laughed.

I was glad someone found me humorous because, lately, I had been feeling like shit. I had lost my best friend and the man I loved all in one day. I had known it would be a risk, telling Griffin how I felt. I'd stupidly thought that my love would pull him out of his grief enough for him to realize that he had something else to live for.

Every day, I asked myself if I could have done some-thing differently, and I still didn't have an answer. I knew I couldn't continue with him and the way things had been. I had been so exhausted, and I would have come to resent him if things had gone on.

Thankfully, due to our mutual friends, I had heard that Griffin had plateaued for a while. Christina had told me that there hadn't been any more fights, and just last week, Blake had gotten Griffin out of bed. It seemed Griffin was on the mend, although Christina had warned me it would probably be a slow process.

Which was why I had decided not to contact him yet. I wanted so badly to let him know I was thinking about him, but part of me was worried that I would set him back. It was probably an irrational fear, but it was still a fear, and I couldn't shake it.

Besides, if he was doing so well, then he could contact me. After all, he was the one who had kicked me out of his apartment, never to be heard from again.

"You okay, Madeline?" Hope asked.

I blinked. "Wow. Sorry. I think I spaced out there for a minute."

She smiled sympathetically. "I heard things have been rough with Griffin."

"Yeah." I nudged her and smiled. "Thanks for finding me a replacement though."

She frowned. "I didn't find you a replacement."

"Oh. Well, I guess since I'm walking down with Troy's cousin, Troy found the replacement." I shrugged. "You still did most of the planning."

"Hope?" Christina called from the hallway. "Has Madeline arrived yet?" She stopped in the doorway when she saw me. "Oh, you're already here."

I ran over to her and gave her a hug. "Happy wedding day eve."

I supposed now that Griffin was out of the picture, Christina was my best friend. I wondered if she knew she had large shoes to fill.

"Why are you looking at me like that?" she asked.

I laughed. "No reason. Just thinking about how glad I am to have you in my life."

Christina looked around me at her sister. "Hope, did you give Madeline something?"

"Ha-ha. No, I'm not on anything. And shouldn't we hurry before we're late?" I stepped around Christina. "I'm looking forward to meeting some cousins."

Christina ran up behind me. "Cousins?"

"Yeah." I lowered my voice. "Your evil cousin, Chantel, and—"

Christina groaned. "Oh. Her."

"Will I know who she is?"

Christina and Hope laughed.

"Oh, you'll know," Christina said.

I rubbed my hands together. "I can't wait. Don't worry. I'll do my best to make sure she doesn't ruin anything."

"Aw, you're so sweet."

"I'm also looking forward to meeting my new aisle mate. Please tell me Troy's cousin is tall, dark, and handsome."

Christina's smile slipped. "About that…"

It was my turn to groan. "Oh God. So, you're saying he's short, pale, and ugly." I waved my hand through the air. "That's okay. It was wishful thinking."

"That's not what I was going to say," Christina said as we made our way to the foyer, right outside of the room where the services would be held, where the rest of the wedding party had gathered. "It's about—"

"Ladies and gentlemen, thank you all for being here. I know Troy and Christina appreciate it. I'm Pastor Lutz, and I am honored to officiate the wedding."

As Pastor Lutz talked, I felt someone come up behind me. I looked over my shoulder to see a beautiful blonde woman who was dressed up like she was going to a fashion show. The rest of the wedding party was wearing jeans, T-shirts, and sweatshirts. Even the pastor was wearing jeans. This woman had to be cousin Chantel.

"Bridesmaids, maid of honor, best man, and grooms-men, can you line up?" Pastor Lutz asked, and Hope instructed us on the order we were assigned to stand in.

"This is the door you will enter the sanctuary through. All the guests will be seated before you all line up. Once we get to the front, we'll go through the next steps. Troy, you can go inside. Christina, you and your dad get behind the bridesmaids."

"*I'm last?*" a high-pitched female voice whined. It was the blonde woman. "But Aunt Deedee said I was second."

Now, I knew it was Chantel. Deedee was Christina's mom.

"There must have been a mix-up, Chantel," Hope said. "Madeline and Griffin are second because they introduced Christina and Troy."

I flinched at hearing Griffin's name, but I figured Chantel was not the person to explain to that it originally was going to be Griffin but that he had needed to be replaced. Best to stick with basic facts with someone like her.

Chantel looked at Christina, who shrugged. Christina's father was next to her, and he rolled his eyes. Apparently, everyone felt the same way about this particular cousin.

I turned away to hide my laughter. It was just a wedding. Who cared what order people walked in? I would volunteer to switch, except Christina didn't want me to.

The groomsmen lined up next to the bridesmaids, and the best man stood next to the maid of honor, but I was all alone. Chantel had distracted me, and I had forgotten to watch for an unfamiliar face.

Everyone was starting to quiet down now that we were all in place.

I leaned forward and whispered, "Hope, what happened to Troy's cousin?"

She turned around. "Oh, Madeline, I think you're confused. You're not walking with Troy's cousin."

I frowned. "I'm not? Who am I walking with?"

A cold gust blew around us as the door to the church opened from outside.

A deep voice that I would know anywhere said, "I'm here. I'm here." Griffin jogged up to me and smiled. "Sorry I'm late."

Meanwhile, I could only stare.

THIRTY-SEVEN

MADELINE

I DIDN'T EVEN HAVE a chance to say anything to Griffin because as soon as he arrived at my side, Pastor Lutz began directing the group to their places.

When we reached the front of the church, Griffin went to the groom's side while I went to the bride's.

I tried to focus on Christina and the pastor, but my mind was going a hundred miles a minute.

What is Griffin doing here? Why didn't anyone tell me he was going to be here? Why hadn't I heard from him? Why didn't anyone tell me he was going to be here? How does he look so healthy, like nothing happened? Why didn't anyone tell me he was going to be here!

I knew I'd kept thinking the same thing on repeat, but it was an important question.

As Pastor Lutz went over how things were going to work, I kept glancing at Griffin out of the corner of my eye. He caught me once and smiled like the last few months hadn't happened.

I quickly darted my eyes away.

"Okay, let's run through this one more time from the

beginning," Pastor Lutz said. "But before we do that, we're going to practice walking out. Troy and Christina, lead the way, and, Troy, you'll come back in here once you reach the foyer."

When Griffin and I met up again, I hesitantly put my arm through the crook of his. Somehow, I'd been in such shock on my walk up to the altar that I had missed how good he looked and how incredible he smelled. His scent brought up more memories than I had been prepared for, and I realized for the millionth time how much I'd missed him.

"How have you been?" he asked me.

I chuckled in disbelief. So, that was how it was between us now. *Unbelievable.*

"Fine," I said.

"Madeline, I've known you a long time. You are the opposite of fine when you say it like that."

We reached the front and turned around to go back into the church. I ignored Griffin and prayed we'd go back inside soon.

"I wanted to say thank you for helping me out after my dad's death."

I started tapping my foot, and I refused to look at him. I didn't want to hear *thank you* like I was some acquaintance. I wanted to hear that he'd missed me.

I wanted to hear that he was in love with me too.

Oh God. Why are we just standing here?

"Madeline, please talk to me."

I was beginning to think he wasn't going to give this up.

I turned to him and whispered sharply, "Not now, Griffin. We are in the middle of a wedding rehearsal. A rehearsal that I didn't even know you were going to be at, okay? Now's not the time to talk. You're just going to have to wait."

I spun away from him before he could answer, and Pastor Lutz picked that very moment to have us enter the church again.

Thank God.

GRIFFIN

It took me a minute to locate Christina after the rehearsal was over, but I finally found her in a corner, having a heated conversation with her sister and some blonde woman.

I was about to turn around and leave until their chat was over, but Christina's eyes lit up when she saw me.

"Griffin?" She rushed over to me. "Is there something I can help you with?"

"Have you seen Madeline? She said she had to use the restroom after the pastor was finished with us, and now, I can't find her. I hope she didn't drown in there."

Christina didn't laugh at my joke, and the light she had in her eyes dimmed. "She left, Griffin."

"What? But I thought she would be at the rehearsal dinner."

"She planned to be, but she said she had to go take care of something and left." She crossed her arms over her chest. "But I think we know that was a lie. You didn't tell her that you were going to be here today, did you?"

I frowned. "I thought you would have told to her. I

wanted to talk to her in person. I did not want to do it through text."

"And look how that turned out for you."

"Are you mad at me?"

"I'm not happy with you." She sighed and dropped her arms. "You basically ghosted her after your father died, and we all understand. You were grieving. But while you were holed up in your apartment, Madeline's life continued. And now that you're better, you waltz in here and expect everything to go back to the way things were. You didn't want to tell her in a text that you were going to be in the wedding again? Fine. You know where she lives. You know where she works. And you know her phone number." She shook her head. "I told Troy to tell you that I wasn't going to be the one to break the news to her, but I should have known you hadn't said anything when she didn't bring it up to me. I'd been so consumed with the wedding, so I assumed she was okay with seeing you again." She leaned closer to me. "By the way, it's one thing to ghost your supposed best friend, but it's another to ghost the woman you're sleeping with."

"You know we slept together?"

"Yeah. After she kept crying every time I mentioned your name, I finally dug that little tidbit out of her." Christina shook her head. "I'm disappointed in you, Griffin."

"I…I thought—" I ran my hand through my hair. "Dammit. I don't know. I thought I would walk in here, and she would be so happy to see me, and we'd…"

"Live happily ever after?" Christina laughed.

She stopped when she saw the wince on my face.

"Wow. And I thought women were hopeless romantics."

"I guess Madeline made me watch one too many romantic comedies."

Christina patted my chest. "You're not in a movie, buddy, and just seeing your face is not going to fix everything. You owe Madeline a real apology." She looked at me sympathetically and walked away.

Shit, shit, shit. I had planned to apologize. If only I hadn't been late, I could have pulled Madeline aside and talked to her.

Now, she was probably even madder at me.

I sure as hell needed to figure out what I was going to do about that.

THIRTY-EIGHT

MADELINE

I SIPPED my drink as I picked at my appetizer. Not only had I lost my best friend and the man I loved, but I'd also lost my favorite bar to hang out in. I missed going to My Favorite Place. Not only to see Griffin's face, but I had made friends with his bartenders and some of the regulars too.

Casey and I had texted back and forth a few times, but it wasn't the same as seeing her several times a week.

So far, I hadn't found a good replacement for My Favorite Place, and I always felt lonely, coming to a bar by myself. I'd never felt that way, going to Griffin's bar. Tonight, I should have probably gone home instead, but that would have made me feel even lonelier since I was missing the rehearsal dinner.

"Madeline? Is that you?"

I turned my attention in the direction I'd heard my name. "Oh, hi, Harris."

I hadn't seen my ex-boyfriend since Griffin had basically kicked him out of my house.

I looked around. "Who are you here with?"

He came over and leaned against the bar. "Some coworkers."

"Oh yeah, it's Friday."

"You had the day off, I take it?"

"Christina and Troy are getting married tomorrow, and this afternoon was the rehearsal. You remember them, right?" I joked.

Harris looked sheepish. "Yes, I remember them. And I'm sorry I never gave them a chance."

I leaned way back and then forward and squinted my eyes. "Are you really Harris?"

He chuckled. "Yes. Now that we're not together anymore, I can see where I went wrong."

"How grown-up of you."

"I'm trying."

I didn't know what I was thinking, but I held my hand out to the seat next to me. "Would you like to sit? Or are your coworkers waiting?"

He smiled. "I can sit for a bit." He pulled up the stool. "And just so we're clear, I'm not taking all the blame in our relationship," he joked.

I laughed. "I never thought you would." I picked up my drink and took the last sip.

"Can I buy you a drink?" he asked, eyeing my glass.

"Yes, please."

Harris raised his hand to the bartender.

"So, because my first airplane needed maintenance before we could take off, I missed my layover flight. I had to sit in the airport for five hours, waiting for the next plane, for which I was only on standby, which means I wasn't even guaranteed a seat." Harris took a sip of his drink. "I told my boss that I was never flying over the holidays again."

I laughed so hard that I fell against him. If I had been sober, I wouldn't have found the story so funny, but thankfully, I was a happy drunk tonight.

I sat up and looked Harris in the eyes. "We used to have good times, right?"

He smiled. "In the beginning, we had a lot of good times, if I remember correctly."

My face heated and turned away. Sex with Harris was nothing compared to sex with Griffin, but it had still been enjoyable.

"Sometimes, I wish I had never broken up with you."

Harris cleared his throat. "Come again?"

I sighed and fiddled with my drink, swirling it around, tipping my cup back and forth. "If I had never broken up with you, I would never have asked Griffin to have sex with me on my birthday, and then I would never have fallen in love with him."

"Are things not going well? I was wondering where he was and why you were here."

I smiled sadly at Harris. "We had a falling-out. I'd stupidly thought I wouldn't fall for Griff, but I did. Then, I'd stupidly thought if I told him how I felt, he'd tell me he felt the same way." I shrugged. "Part of it's my fault. I told him after his father passed away."

Harris sucked in a breath through his teeth. "Oh, Madeline, that's rough."

"Yeah. I didn't hold it against him though. I gave him

his space, thinking he'd come back to me." I tipped my glass back and swallowed the rest of my drink. "I hadn't seen him in over a month, and he just showed up at the rehearsal and acted like we were old acquaintances."

"Ah...I was wondering why you weren't at their rehearsal dinner, but I didn't want to pry."

I put my elbow on the bar and my head on my hand. "I bailed after the rehearsal was over." I sat up straight. The angry drunk was coming out. "Which pisses me off. He should have been the one to leave. I wasn't the one who had disappeared for weeks on end. He should be the one avoiding *me*. He should have been the one to skip out on the dinner. He should be the one sitting alone in a bar, feeling sorry for himself." I reached for my purse and started digging through it.

"What are you doing?"

"Trying to find my phone."

"Dare I ask, why?"

"So, I can call and give Griffin a piece of my mind."

Harris put his hand on mine. "Now, I'm obviously not a relationship expert. But he's still your best friend, and you still care about him, right?"

I nodded.

"Then, I'm thinking you should wait until tomorrow to talk to him." He squeezed my hand. "Let me take you home. You can have a good night's sleep and call him in the morning."

"Okay," I said reluctantly.

He looked relieved. "Let me go and tell my coworkers I'm going to take off. Do you have someone who can give you a ride to pick up your car in the morning? Otherwise, I can drive your car and ask one of them to follow."

"I'll be fine. My mom can give me a ride if I need one."

Harris stood. "I'll be right back. Don't go anywhere."

"Aye, aye, captain."

He chuckled. "You really are drunk."

I shrugged. It was the truth.

As soon as Harris was out of earshot, I pulled my phone out of my purse and dialed Griffin.

"Come on, come on, answer," I said into the ringing phone. I didn't want Harris to come back and catch me.

Griffin's stupid voice mail picked up.

"Hey, Griffin. This is Madeline. Remember me? Your former best friend." My words were starting to slur, so I cleared my throat and firmed up my voice. "I'm just calling to tell you that you should have been the one to leave tonight. It's not right that you got to stay with our friends. You're the one who ditched me. You're the one who forgot about me. And you should have been the one to go home alone tonight."

I had been keeping an eye out for Harris and saw him coming back.

"But you know what? I don't need you. Harris is taking me home, and tomorrow, I'm going to pretend like I never loved you. In fact, I'm going to pretend like you and I were never friends. So, stay away from me."

Harris was getting close.

"Gotta go. Harris is almost here."

I clicked End and set my phone down.

"Who was that?" Harris asked.

"Umm…" I gasped as an idea came to me. "It was my

mom." I nodded. "Mmhmm. I was just making sure she could help me pick up my car tomorrow."

He looked at my phone, so I snatched it up and stuck it in my purse.

"Are you ready?" I asked, hopping off my stool. I swayed and fell against him. I burst out laughing. "Whoops."

"Someone is happy again," he said, helping me stand up straight.

"Yep." I always felt better after getting stuff off my chest.

THIRTY-NINE
GRIFFIN

AS I SAT in my vehicle, I listened to Madeline's message again.

I didn't know why I was torturing myself with it because Madeline had not answered her phone when I called her back. And I had only missed her call by ten minutes.

Which was why I was now sitting in her driveway, praying that she showed up. It had already been five minutes, and considering she'd had a head start, I was beginning to worry that she had gone to Harris's house.

The idea filled me with dread. If I had driven her back into the arms of that asshole, I was never going to forgive myself. At least this way, if the two of them came back to her house, I might be able to stop her from making a drunken mistake.

Because she had clearly been drinking when she called me.

Just when I thought I was going to bust my steering wheel with all my tension, a car pulled up beside mine.

I turned off my engine and jumped out into the cold weather as Harris opened his door.

"I'm not letting you sleep with her while she's drunk," I told him. "She's not in the right mind to make decisions like that."

He scowled at me. "I wasn't going to sleep with her. I am simply bringing her home. Like a *gentleman*."

I held up my hands. "Sorry. Seriously."

He walked around to the passenger side. "She fell asleep, so you're going to have to come and get her."

I rushed over as he touched the door handle.

"Also, I don't know what you did, but you're lucky she still cares about you. And it's only because I know how close you are that I am leaving her here with you."

I balked. "I would never hurt her."

"Not physically, but the next time I run into her alone in a bar, I'm going to tell her to run as far away from you as she can."

"I know I have some making up to do. That's why I'm here." *And to make sure she doesn't sleep with you.*

Harris nodded. "Good." He opened the door and leaned inside. "Madeline, you're home. It's time to wake up."

"I'm home? Oh. How nice."

Harris backed up. "Come on now. Let me help you up."

Madeline put her hand in his and stood. She squinted when she saw me and then smiled. "Griffin. You're here."

I blinked and looked at Harris. "I thought she was mad at me."

He led her around the open door. "Her moods have been flipping back and forth tonight. Give her a minute, and

I'm sure she'll be mad at you again." He put her hand in mine.

"Gee, thanks."

The two of us walked Madeline up to her door. While I wanted Harris gone, I couldn't help but be thankful. If she slipped on the ice or snow, it would be nice to have someone help me get her into the house.

When we reached the front door, he squeezed her shoulders. "Good night, Madeline."

"Good night, Harris. Thanks for the ride home."

He looked at me. "Don't fuck this up," he said and took off.

"Madeline, where are your keys?"

She held up her purse and waved it in front of me. "In my purse."

I reached for it, and she pulled it away from me and laughed.

"Madeline."

She did it again.

Thankfully, I was quick, and I got it on the third time as she fell against me.

"Griffin, why do you smell so good?" She rubbed her face on my chest where my coat had come down as I dug through her stuff to find her keys.

I found them just as she went on her tippy-toes and licked my neck.

"Jesus Christ." I quickly unlocked the door and gently pushed her inside as I flipped on a light.

Madeline was giggling as she came toward me again.

I stopped her with my hands on her shoulders. "Oh no. We're not doing that again."

She had felt too good against me, and I needed to make sure I didn't do anything stupid tonight, like sleep with her.

She stuck out her lower lip. "Don't you want me, Griff?"

I groaned. "More than you can possibly know. But you are going to bed, young lady."

"Young lady?" She bit her lip. "Are we role-playing?" She turned around and pushed her butt out. "Are you going to spank me for being a bad girl?"

I shook my head and walked toward her bedroom in hopes that she'd follow. "I think you're trying to kill me," I muttered.

I heard her shoes drop on the floor as she ran after me, but I was ready for her. I handed her the biggest, fluffiest pair of pajamas I could find in her dresser. "Go in the bathroom and put these on."

"Wouldn't you rather I take my clothes off right here?" she asked innocently.

"No. Go change."

She wrinkled her nose. "You're no fun."

"I know." I pointed to the bathroom. "Go."

I went into the kitchen, grabbed a tall glass, and filled it with water. Then, I dug through the cabinet for ibuprofen and poured a couple into my hand.

Before I walked back into her room, I peeked my head in to make sure she wasn't naked. I sighed with relief when she walked out of the bathroom in her pajamas.

"Hey, I got you some medicine and water, so hopefully, you don't wake up with a headache."

She did not need a hangover on the day of her friend's wedding.

Thankfully, it wasn't even ten at night, so she should be able to get a good chunk of sleep.

She took the pills and drank all the water before climbing into bed.

I pulled up the covers and tucked her in up to her chin. "You and I will talk in the morning."

She frowned. "So, no sex?"

"No, Mads, no sex."

"Bummer."

FORTY
MADELINE

I SAT on the edge of my bed, feeling out of sorts as I tried to recall the night before. I remembered drinking with Harris—cringe—and actually telling him I wished I hadn't broken up with him—double cringe.

But after that, it was a blur, which was surprising because I didn't have a headache, although I didn't feel one hundred percent either.

I looked down at my PJs. At least I knew I hadn't done something stupid, like have sex with my ex, but he must have picked out what I was wearing because I didn't sleep in this pair of pajamas. They were usually too hot, and I couldn't sleep well.

I guessed I just needed several drinks to go with these PJs if I wanted to wear them to bed. I hadn't woken up once last night.

I pushed myself off the bed and paused, worried the change in elevation would hurt my head or make me dizzy, but all I had to do was pee.

After going to the bathroom, I brushed my teeth and

headed out to the kitchen for some coffee. I came to a screeching halt when I saw Griffin sleeping on my couch.

And that was when the rest of the night came back to me.

The angry phone call, Griffin apparently helping me get into my house, me trying to have sex with him.

Ugh.

So, not only did he know that he'd broken my heart, thanks to my message, but he'd also probably figured out that I hadn't had sex since him.

I marched over to him and repeatedly poked him in the shoulder.

He reached behind him and grabbed my hand. "Ow. That hurts."

I pulled my hand away. "Good."

Griffin rolled over and sat up. As he did, the blanket fell down, and his bare chest was on display.

I felt a twinge between my legs and cursed my vagina.

Thankfully, he was rubbing his eyes and didn't catch me staring longingly at his gorgeous body.

I looked over his shoulder. "What are you doing here?"

"Making sure you're okay."

"I am. You're free to leave now."

"Not until we talk. Or at least, until I talk. All I'm asking you to do is listen."

I didn't want to listen to him, but I also didn't want to keep being mad, especially on Christina and Troy's wedding day.

"Mads, please look at me."

I slowly met his eyes. His were filled with pain, and I didn't want to hear about him being hurt.

So, I jumped him.

My lips landed on his as I straddled him. He kissed me with such passion that it took my breath away. And as he grew hard between my legs, I rubbed my cleft over him.

He drew his mouth away. "Are you still drunk?"

"No." I kissed his neck and ran my hands all over his chest.

He threaded his fingers through my hair and pulled my head up and away from him. "Are you sure this is a good idea? We need to talk. I know you're upset, and I need to apologize."

"If you don't fuck me right now, I promise I'll never forgive you."

Griffin smiled and kissed me again. He threw me down on the couch and yanked my pants off. With one quick move, he got up on his knees, drew his boxers down just enough to pull his cock out, and drove inside me.

"Oh shit," I yelled and clutched at his back.

Wrapping an arm under my ass, he thrust inside me like a man possessed. He angled my hips in the exact right way so that he rubbed his dick precisely where I needed it to be.

"Baby, I'm not going to last long," he said in my ear. "I haven't done this since you left."

I knew Griffin had been in a depressive state after his dad passed, but for some reason, a part of me had pictured him getting freaky with women. Finding out that he hadn't been with anyone since me was the thing I needed to tip me over the edge, and I exploded.

Since I hadn't had an orgasm in a while, I came so hard that I could barely breathe, and I could feel myself getting wetter.

"Fuck me," Griffin said and slammed into me as his climax took hold of his body. His cock jerked, and his seed was hot as he poured into me.

"Oh my God. I needed that," I said. I pushed on his shoulders. "You can get off of me now."

He didn't look happy, but he pulled out of me and sat up.

I grabbed my pajama pants off the floor and pulled them on before I got up.

Griffin ran his hand over his hair. "Can I talk to you now?"

I leaned back on the couch and folded my hands on my chest. "Sure." I was so post-climax relaxed that I probably would have let someone drive a bulldozer through my living room. "You have a limited amount of time before this orgasm haze wears off. Then, I'm kicking your ass out."

When he didn't say anything, I turned my head and looked at him.

He was grinning like a fool.

I pushed his shoulder. "Don't get too full of yourself. I haven't had an orgasm in a long time."

His grin got impossibly bigger.

"Forget I said anything. Talk."

He rubbed his hands together. "First, I owe you a huge thanks."

I clenched my jaw. He was thanking me again.

His hand went up. "I know friends help each other out, but you went above and beyond, Mads. I would be deep in the hole with the bar, and I would have lost a ton of customers if I hadn't had you. And if it makes you feel better, I have spread my thanks out to everyone who helped me. I have realized how incredibly lucky I am to have great friends and family."

"Well, you're welcome, I guess." I narrowed my eyes and lifted my finger. "Don't go thinking you're special or anything. I would have helped anyone in your situation."

He grabbed my finger and brought my hand to his chest. "Now, Mads, we both know that's not true. I'm your best friend."

"Not anymore."

"You're still mine." He linked our hands together and kissed the back of mine. "And I am so sorry that I hurt you. As you can probably guess, I was not in my right mind. You know I was close with my dad. And I still can't believe he's —" His voice choked.

I squeezed his hand.

"I still can't believe he's gone."

"Oh, Griff." I turned sideways. "I hope you know I'm not upset that you were depressed after what happened to your dad. Because I'm not. I'm not even that upset that when I told you I couldn't do it anymore, you didn't really care. And I'm also not that upset that I told you I loved you and you slammed the door in my face. I was—and still am —hurt, but I'm not mad at you. What I'm angry about is that you are doing better, and not once did you contact me." I lifted a shoulder. "I thought when you were feeling ready, I'd be the first person you called."

"Listen, I don't know how much you heard, but even though I got out of bed, it took me a while before I got myself on the right track. I've been going to a grief support group, and I started seeing a therapist. And then all my other time has been devoted to me getting back into the bar.

I had so much to catch up on while I was grieving. I don't know if anyone told you, but I didn't even know how much time had passed."

My heart went out to him. "I'm sorry," I whispered.

He shook his head. "No sorrys. It's not your fault. But anyway, I feel like all I've been doing is working, doing therapy, and sleeping. I've been working very hard to get my life back on track before yesterday."

"Why yesterday?"

"Because I knew I was going to see you. And, Mads, I had no idea you didn't know I was coming until yesterday when Christina yelled at me. I guess she gave Troy directions to pass on to me, that I had to be the one to let you know I was in the wedding again. But I think Troy's exact message to me was, 'Don't forget to text Madeline.' Thanks, buddy. That was real clear."

I covered my mouth as I laughed. "Christina really yelled at you?"

"Kind of. We were at the church with people all around, so yelling is a bit of an exaggeration."

"I would say I'm sorry, but you told me not to."

Griffin laughed and shook his head. "That, and I deserved it, huh?"

"Just a little bit," I said, holding up my finger and thumb close together.

"Well, I'm sorry you didn't know I was coming. I'm sorry I hadn't taken the time to tell you, so you weren't blindsided."

"You're forgiven...I suppose," I teased him. "I'm glad that you are getting help."

"Does this mean we can be best friends again?"

I sighed and tried to take my hand back, but he refused to let go. "Griffin, I have missed you more than you know. But…" I looked away. "I don't know if things can just go back to the way they were before." I turned back to him. "I think I'm going to have to take it slow and build back up to being just friends again."

He tilted his head and opened his mouth, but then he closed it again before he said anything.

"Are you okay?"

He nodded sluggishly and pointed to the couch. "You know we just had sex, right?"

I slapped my free hand over my eyes. "And you didn't want to. Now, it's my turn to apologize."

Prying my fingers off my face, he asked, "Are you purposely being obtuse?"

"I don't think so."

"You know I wanted to have sex with you as much as you wanted to have it with me, right? Probably more."

"I suppose that's good news."

"I would like to think so, yes." He studied my face. "I sense a but coming."

"But…I can't go back to being friends with benefits with you, Griff." I closed my eyes. *Am I really going to put myself out there again?* It appeared so. I opened them and took a deep breath. "I love you, Griffin. I am still in love with you. I can be your friend—with time, as I said before—or I can be your girlfriend, but I can't be something in between." I shook my head. "At least, not at this time in my life. It hurts too much."

He tugged me forward, and I screeched as I landed on my back in his lap.

"Then, that is all my fault because I love you too, Madeline. I'm sorry I didn't say it weeks ago, but you honestly caught me by surprise, and…let's face it…I wasn't ready." He smiled down at me. "But I am now. I don't think I was clear when I said I was working hard to get my life back on track these last few weeks before I saw you again. I wanted to make sure that I was worthy of you loving me."

"Oh, Griff." I threw my arms around him. "I love you so much."

He leaned down and kissed me. "I love you too, baby. More than you'll ever know."

FORTY-ONE
MADELINE

"SO, you and Griffin made up, huh?" Christina asked me as we took a break from dancing at her wedding reception and stood on the sidelines.

I smiled. *Oh, we made up all right.* "Yes."

"I'm so glad because you two belong together. And I've been waiting years for you both to realize it."

My mouth fell open. "Why have you never told me this?"

"Because I didn't want to influence you at all. Your relationship had to progress naturally."

"I think marriage has gone to your head. You think you're a romance guru now," I joked.

"You're funny," she said sarcastically. "But seriously, in my head, I always pictured the two of you ending up together."

"It looks like you might have been right."

"I love being right."

I laughed. "I hope your new husband knows that about you."

She laughed, too, and put her hand on my arm. "And I'm sorry you didn't know about Griffin yesterday. I thought you knew and didn't want to talk about it. Even so, I should have asked you if you were okay."

I put my hand on hers. "It's fine. I heard there was a communication mix-up."

"Yeah, never send a man to relay a serious message to another man."

I laughed again. "It's true. And it's really okay. You were in the middle of planning a wedding, and I don't blame you." I shrugged. "Maybe it's even good that I didn't know because it didn't give me time to obsess about it."

"But you missed dinner last night."

"I'm sorry about that."

"Don't be sorry. I just feel bad. Although it wasn't that exciting."

"Griffin told me Chantel complained the whole time."

Christina gritted her teeth. "Boy, did she ever. Hope took her aside and told her if she complained one time today, she would be kicked out of the wedding party entirely."

"Aw." I put my hand over my heart. "Sisters are the best."

"They really are. And some cousins are not." She pointed to the cake table, where Chantel stood a little too close to Griffin. "I'd get over there before she offers herself up as dessert."

"I doubt that," I told Christina.

"I'm not joking."

"Okay, okay, I'll go." But as I walked over, it felt good to know I wasn't worried.

When I reached them, Griffin looked over his shoulder at me and grinned.

I loved that I was the one to make him smile like that.

He held his arm out, and I slid into his embrace.

"Hey, Chantel, did you ever get a chance to meet my girlfriend, Madeline?"

Chantel pursed her lips. "Not really."

"Yeah, sorry, I had to leave before dinner last night." I held out my hand. "It's nice to meet you."

She shook it, but she didn't seem happy about it. "Same to you."

"Do you mind if I steal my boyfriend for a bit?" A slow song came on at that exact second. "I want to dance with him."

She rolled her eyes. "Sure. Whatever."

Taking Griffin's hand, I led him out to the dance floor. He spun me around and then pulled me into his arms, and we began to sway to the music.

I laid my head on his chest. I knew that not everything would be perfect between us, but at that moment, I was so happy that my heart felt like it was bursting.

"Did I tell you that you look beautiful today?"

I smiled. "Yes. Several times."

"Did I tell you that, as we were walking up the aisle, a part of me wished it were our wedding?"

I jerked my head up. "What?"

He laughed. "I know. We haven't been together but a minute, but the thing is, we've known each other forever. And I know that I want to be with you till the end of time."

My eyes widened. "Are you proposing to me?"

"Huh, I guess I kind of am."

I wrapped my arms around his neck. "I want to spend the rest of my life with you, too, but today is not the day."

He frowned. "Why not?"

"Because today is Christina's day."

"What about Troy?"

"Troy shmoy. We all know it's the bride's day."

"Okay, I'll give you that."

"Anyway, it's Christina's day, and I'm not going to get engaged on her wedding day. Besides, you don't have a ring."

Griffin wiggled his eyebrows. "What if I told you I did?"

I stopped breathing. There was no way he'd actually bought one.

"I'd call you a liar."

He lifted a shoulder. "I guess you'll never know."

"You're such a tease. But since we just got back together, why don't you wait a month? If you still want to marry me, you can get down on one knee and ask."

He kissed me long and hard. "You got yourself a deal. I'll ask. You just wait and see."

And one month to the day, he did.

EPILOGUE

MADELINE

I GRABBED Griffin's hand as the plane began to land while I stared out the window. "I can't believe when we step out of here, we're finally going to be in Europe." I turned my head and looked at my husband.

He leaned over and kissed me. "Happy thirty-fifth birthday, baby."

I snagged his shirt in my fist. "You know that all I need is you, right? But Europe sure is nice."

He smiled at me, and fifteen minutes later, we were walking down the jet bridge and into the airport.

As soon as we were out in the open, I pulled out my phone, turned it off Airplane Mode, and hoped my international phone plan worked. When I didn't get a signal right away, I stopped walking and held up the cell.

Griffin noticed I wasn't beside him, spun around, and came back to me. "Mads, what are you doing?"

"Just calling our moms."

He sighed and hung his head in defeat. "Babe, we were in the air for, like, eleven hours. It hasn't been that long since we left them. I think when you told me that all you needed for your birthday was me, you meant, me and the kids."

Aha. A signal. I dialed my mom's number and put the phone to my ear.

I tugged on my husband's shirt. "Of course, you and the kids. But they're not here."

He threw his hands up and went to find the nearest chair.

Ten minutes later, after I was assured that all my babies were safe and sound, I walked over to Griffin. "Okay, I'm ready."

He looked up from his phone. "For someone who had to postpone her birthday trip for five years, I'm surprised we're still sitting here."

"Technically, I'm standing, but you know, if someone hadn't gotten me pregnant, we could have gone when we were supposed to."

He looked around. "Who got you pregnant? Because it sure wasn't me."

I grabbed his hand and pulled him up. "Right, I only gave birth to the mini version of you, but someone else got me pregnant."

He grinned and threw his arm around me. "Yeah, Levi looks like me, huh?"

I rolled my eyes. "He sure does. And if you must know, he asked my mom where Daddy was about five hundred times and only asked for Mommy, like, twice."

He kissed my shoulder. "I'm sorry, babe. You know that Zoey will ask for you once she can talk."

I snorted. "Yeah, right. We'll see."

"Well, until then, how about we enjoy our well-earned vacation?"

I smiled at my husband. "You're right. Let's. But before we do, are you sure you don't have to call the bar just to check if everything's okay?"

"You think you're so funny, but I have left things in the capable hands of my employees and friends."

I put my hand on his chest. "I'm proud of you, you know."

His eyebrows flew up. "Oh?"

"Yeah. Back when you gave me those tickets for my thirtieth birthday, I really didn't think you'd leave the bar for so long."

"Well, babe, I've learned that there are more important things than my business. Yes, it helps put food on our table and keep a roof over our heads, but you and the kids are what really matters. And if I have to fly halfway around the world in order to make love to my wife without someone interrupting us, then I will do it."

"So, this trip is about you and your dick?"

"Nah. It's all about you. My dick just gets to reap the benefits." He looked sheepish. "And full disclosure: I did send some texts while you were on the phone."

I playfully smacked his chest. "Oh, Griff."

We made it to baggage claim and waited for our luggage to be spit out. "I love you, Griffin. Thanks for bringing me here."

He kissed me. "I love you too. And the pleasure is all mine."

MY GUY PROBLEM SAMPLE

LYDIA

I had less than a week to figure out how I was going to get out of the mess I had agreed to participate in. But first, I needed to get out of my apartment.

A latte was calling my name.

I stepped out of my apartment just as my neighbor's door opened and his girlfriend walked out.

"Hi, Lydia," she said to me.

"Hi, Rose." I looked at the open door and sneered at my shirtless—but *too hot for his own good*—neighbor. "Broderick."

He smirked at me. "Lydia."

Broderick DeVries—or Brode*dick*, as I liked to call him in my head sometimes—and I did not get along, and I tried to avoid him at all costs. About a month after he'd moved in, our complex had hosted a Super Bowl party in the common area, and he'd told me to my face that the dip I'd brought sucked. It was the first time I had met the guy. He parked in the guest parking all the time, making it hard for actual guests to find a spot sometimes. Also, he liked to play his music loud enough for me to hear it in my apartment. Most of the time, I didn't mind, but it was still rude.

And don't even get me started on all the women who came and went from his place. My heart went out to poor Rose. As someone who could stand to lose five or ten pounds myself, I felt bad for her. I loved my body and actually liked that I had curves, but not all women were as comfortable in their own skin as I was, thanks to stupid diet culture. Rose was on the heavier side and seemed like such a sweet person. Most of the other women I'd seen coming out of Broderick's apartment were thin and attractive, and it appeared as if he preferred thin women.

I guessed I didn't actually know that Rose was his girlfriend, but she was the one I saw most often. Plus, she was clearly in love with Broderick based on the way she practically swooned whenever he said anything. Cheating was just another reason to avoid relationships.

At times, I wanted to tell her that her boyfriend was a liar and a cheater, but I didn't know either of them well enough. And if I told her, would I have to tell all the women? Did they all think they were dating him?

I had no idea, and I didn't want to find out. I wanted to stay as far away from that dumpster fire as I could. I had told a friend once that her fiancé was cheating on her. She had ditched me and married his stupid ass anyway.

Not wanting to get involved was the reason I did the next thing.

"Oh shoot. I forgot something. Bye, Rose."

I didn't want to have to walk down the hall, the stairs,

and out the front door with her and pretend like everything was okay.

I unlocked my door, stepped inside for ten seconds, and then exited again.

"I know you don't like me, but you didn't have to be so rude to Rose," Broderick said.

I clapped my hand against my chest after I finished locking up. "I'm rude?"

"Yeah. Rose is nice, and it wouldn't kill you to be nice back."

I moved closer and tried to keep my eyes off his tan, muscular chest. Why an asshole like him was blessed with such a beautiful body, I didn't know. Not only was he unfaithful, but he also didn't seem to have a job. How could he when he was entertaining ladies all day? Where he got the money to pay for his apartment, I also didn't know. Our rent wasn't cheap, and he had one more bedroom than me. I had to wonder if he was one of those trust-fund babies— but obviously the black sheep of the family.

"I am nice," I said. "And I don't think you should lecture anyone on being rude when the first thing you ever said to me was, 'Your spinach and artichoke dip needs work.' "

He lifted a shoulder and stepped out of his doorway. "Sometimes, the truth hurts, baby."

"Nobody asked you."

"I was trying to save you from embarrassment before everyone in the building ate it."

"Oh yeah, because telling me my cooking needs work in front of all our neighbors wasn't embarrassing at all."

"It wasn't all our neighbors."

I rolled my eyes and inched closer. I jabbed him in the

chest. "That is a lame argument. And maybe you should take your own advice. Rose *is* nice, and it wouldn't kill you to come clean with her."

His brow furrowed. "Come clean with her how?"

"As if you don't know."

He laughed in disbelief. "I don't have a fucking clue as to what you're talking about."

I poked him again. "And that is why I will never like you."

He raised his hands and shook them in mock fear. "Oh no, Lydia doesn't like me." He put his face close to mine, and I couldn't help but notice how green his eyes were in contrast to his bronze skin and his dark hair and beard. "News flash: I don't care. I know everyone else around here thinks you're charming and sweet, but I know you're not."

I gritted my teeth and pursed my lips as I got closer. "I am charming and sweet."

Man, does he always smell this good? No wonder Rose put up with his cheating ass.

For a moment, I let myself picture what it would be like to have sex with Broderick. All those muscles and those intense eyes staring into mine as he——

"Are you okay?" he asked me as he backed away.

I squared my shoulders. "Once I get away from you, I will be perfectly fine."

He swept his arm out. "Nothing's stopping you from leaving, baby."

I went to leave but paused because I liked to have the last word. "Stop calling me baby."

He smirked again. "Now, why would I do that?"

"Because I don't like it."

His eyes looked down at my chest. "Your nipples say otherwise."

I quickly scanned my chest to see both my nipples poking out of my shirt and bra like an indicator on a Thanksgiving turkey.

"Ugh," I groaned and stomped away.

I could hear Broderick laughing all the way down the hall.

It was only after I was on the stairs that I realized I had the perfect comeback.

At least I know how to wear a shirt.

I hated when my retorts came to me too late.

Get My Guy Problem now!

ABOUT THE AUTHOR

R.L. Kenderson is two best friends writing under one name.

Renae has always loved reading, and in third grade, she wrote her first poem where she learned she might have a knack for this writing thing. Lara remembers sneaking her grandmother's Harlequin novels when she was probably too young to be reading them, and since then, she knew she wanted to write her own.

When they met in college, they bonded over their love of reading and the TV show *Charmed*. What really spiced up their friendship was when Lara introduced Renae to romance novels. When they discovered their first vampire romance, they knew there would always be a special place in their hearts for paranormal romance. After being unable to find certain storylines and characteristics they wanted to read about in the hundreds of books they consumed, they decided to write their own.

One lives in the Minneapolis-St. Paul area and the other in the Kansas City area where they both work in the medical field during the day and a sexy author by night. They communicate through phone, email, and whole lot of messaging.

You can find them at http://www.rlkenderson.com, Facebook, Instagram, TikTok, and Goodreads. Join their

Made in the USA
Coppell, TX
25 February 2024

29416946R00144